THE

EVENT

THE EVENT

West Avenue Books

The Event.

Printed in the United States. For information about subsidiary rights go to: rich@richardbognar.com

The characters and events in this book are fictional and any resemblance to actual persons or events is coincidental.

ISBN-978-0-9890962-0-1

Library of Congress Control Number: 2013935000

REMEMBRANCE

West Avenue Books remembers Josephine Delmont, the last of our mothers from West Avenue. We will remember always your kind and gentle smile.

ACKNOWLEDGMENT

First, I want to thank Stephanie Beavers, my editor, for the care and scrutiny she has given to this book. Stephanie has added clarity and conciseness to many of my less than perfect sentences. Secondly, my thanks go to Kimberly Martin at Jera Publishing for providing the mechanical layout of this book, and for her guidance throughout the project. Last, and certainly not least, I want to thank C.J. Barnard for the book cover design. C.J. used acrylic on canvas to create an original piece of art. I am grateful to have these three talented individuals support me during the creation of this book.

For
Cyndy

If not for you none of this would exist.

THE
EVENT

PROLOGUE

Charlie Connolly saw the beauty of the Great Plains. Yellow primroses sprang from rock crevices, and foot-high elephant heads bloomed with bright pink and purple flowers. Goldenrod sprouted from the earth far and wide, and grass types were too numerous to count. In the distance, waves of wheat swayed in the field as far as the eye could see. In the solitude of the moment, Charlie began to whistle "America the Beautiful." A fine rain began to mist the air. Moments later it came down in sheets and forced him back to the car. He opened the door and, before stepping inside, looked back at the massive, beautiful land and tried to envision office buildings and subdivisions where wheat swayed across the endless plains.

CHAPTER ONE

Charlie Connolly, the U.S. senator from New York, was not supposed to lose to his upstart opponent, Mike Adams. Charlie had given it everything he had, but in the end he came up short where it mattered most: votes. The newspaper was less kind. "Connolly gets throttled by Adams." In hindsight, Charlie was no match for his better-financed opponent who had run a textbook negative campaign. Adams painted Charlie as a liar, a money-grabbing politician, and a man you would never want to babysit your twelve-year-old daughter. The camera loved Adams, especially when he shook his finger and said, "Charlie Connolly will strip entitlements from the poor, send jobs overseas, destroy our economy, repeal laws that protect women's bodies, and increase wealth for the wealthy."

In Charlie's speeches, he was less brazen and spoke more about the poor condition of the country. He warned voters they could no longer afford deficit spending of $4 billion a day, and that the national debt would soon reach $20 trillion if an austerity program were not implemented. Charlie's message failed to resonate with voters and Adams won a glowing landslide victory. After the election there was little for Charlie to do except wrap up loose ends and vacate his office so Adams could move into it. All that remained before leaving Washington was an unofficial stop at the White House, at the request of President Backer O'Boyle. The two men had served in the Senate together and, although they belonged to different parties, they had co-sponsored a number of bills and developed a friendship over the years.

"Charlie, when are you heading home?" The president handed him a martini and patted him on the back.

"The car's packed and I'm leaving this evening."

"We'll miss you in Washington, but something tells me you'll be back."

The president flashed his perfect smile. It was one he flashed a hundred times a day, yet it never lost its radiance or appeal.

"Thank you for the sentiment, Mr. President, but I'm retiring from politics."

"Give yourself time to recoup, Charlie. You ran into a buzz-saw with Adams. Once the sting wears off, you'll think differently about it."

Charlie knew the president wasn't ribbing him—he wasn't vicious in that way—but it's always unpleasant to hear how badly you've been drubbed. The only good thing about being invited to the White House was that it gave him the chance to speak his mind. To say what he really thought. "Word on the street is you're going to announce a new tax increase for the middle class. I heard corporations are getting one, too."

"We must all pay our fair share, especially big business. It's time for them to cough up what they owe this nation."

Over a second martini Charlie spoke more freely with the president. "How are you going to cap deficit spending? And, Mr. President, borrowing from the Chinese has to stop."

"Charlie, you worry too much. The economy's going to turn around. As soon as it does, we'll start buying our debt back from China."

"Moody's has threatened to lower our credit rating again. What happens when foreign countries refuse to lend us another dime?"

The president did not answer. Instead, he sipped his martini and looked out the Oval Office window at the newly manicured lawn. Charlie would have given anything to know what he was thinking at that moment, but the telephone rang and the president said he needed to take the call. They shook hands and Charlie received another pat on the back before security arrived to escort him out.

He visited his favorite Italian restaurant where he dined on spaghetti and meatballs. Afterwards, he began to dread the long trip back to New York. Not so much the five-hour drive, but the constant reminder that he had lost his Senate seat. For a politician there could be no greater torture.

CHAPTER TWO

Political campaigns, especially grueling ones, take their toll on a candidate's family. Charlie's wife Angela, and Kaitlin, their eight-year-old daughter, barely survived the exhaustive campaign. Angela was a singer, not what you call a super-star, but she had a respectable fan base at the time she and Charlie were married. During his run for reelection, Charlie asked Angela to place her singing career on hold until after the election. Reluctantly, she agreed not to accept singing engagements, with her only singing taking place in church.

Kaitlin was in grammar school and faced many of the challenges young girls her age do. Recently, the topic was upper braces to pull her teeth together. She objected to what would be a mouthful of metal, but Charlie assured her that eighteen months would pass quickly, and when it was over and done with, she would have the most beautiful smile. Kaitlin trusted that her dad knew best, and the braces were installed a week later.

Charlie was not unaware that his arduous campaign had placed a strain on his marriage. Two months had passed since the campaign and their relationship had not improved. Angela had no idea what was going through Charlie's head.

To her, he appeared depressed most of the time. Meanwhile, she wasted little time reviving her singing career, and moving on with her life. One night, after Kaitlin was put to bed, Angela broke the news to him.

"I can't go on like this any longer, Charlie. We need to spend some time apart."

Those were the last words he ever expected to hear from Angela. Marriage was sacred, and vows should never be broken, no matter how bad things appear.

"Is there someone else?"

Chapter Three

Charlie stood at the bar with a piña colada in hand and looked out over the swimming pool at Acapulco Bay. Behind him was the Princess Resort Hotel, a spectacular getaway spot according to Robert Devins, his former senatorial aide. It was he who recommended Charlie join him on a short trip to Mexico. Vacations can snap a person out of their depression, he told Charlie.

To Robert's dismay, he became unemployed the day Charlie lost his bid for reelection. He was an attorney, a whiz at constitutional law, but on the other hand, he was still young and carefree, and with no urgent need to find employment. Having been raised in Westchester with the proverbial silver spoon in his mouth gave him the luxury to be able to take his time. While working for Charlie in Washington, some considered Robert a bit frivolous and somewhat scattered at times, but try to trample the rights of people on Main Street, the working class, or the poor, he had the skills to grind those opponents into mincemeat.

"What do you say we find a *langouste* joint?"

Charlie was slow to react. "Sure, let's go eat."

They found a restaurant a mile down the strip. Instead of ordering lobster, Charlie selected scallops. He lacked the patience to crack open a crustacean, mostly because his mind was still on what had occurred back in New York—Angela had left their home and taken Kaitlin with her.

"What do you say we go out tonight, Charlie? I heard there's a swinging dance club not far from the hotel." Robert was single, good looking and raring to go. He enjoyed meeting beautiful women, and Acapulco was loaded with them.

"Think I'll call it a night after dinner, if you don't mind." Charlie had no place hanging around a dance club, and any fantasy about getting lucky had disappeared years ago. If he was going to expend his energy, it would be figuring out how to get Angela back.

Robert went his way and Charlie returned to the hotel. His room was on an upper floor and had a balcony that overlooked Acapulco Bay. A beautiful moon was out and the sky was full of stars. The only thing missing was Angela.

The cell phone rang and Charlie answered it without looking at caller ID. He assumed it was Angela because of the number of messages he'd left for her.

"Angela?"

"No, Charlie. It's Max Plummer."

"Hey, Max. How are you?"

"You sound a little down."

"No, it must be the connection. I'm in Acapulco. What can I do for you?" Max was the CEO of Penfield Oil and Drilling, and also a contributor to Charlie's reelection campaign. Before serving in Congress, Charlie was an attorney and had negotiated drilling rights in the Gulf of Mexico for Penfield.

"I need you back in New York. It's important."

"What's going on?"

"I can't discuss it on the phone. Charlie! Just get here!"

* * *

The red eye arrived in New York's LaGuardia Airport the next morning. Charlie took a taxi straight to Penfield's corporate office on Park Avenue. The receptionist led him into the board room where he counted a dozen or so men seated around the conference table. Max motioned Charlie to his end of the table where an empty chair awaited. Max started the meeting by introducing each of the men at the table. To Charlie's surprise, each was CEO of a Fortune 500 company. Max motioned to his attorney who placed a non-disclosure agreement in front of Charlie. "You need to sign this before we get started."

Charlie scanned the document. "A twenty-page non-disclosure and you expect me to read and sign it now?"

"Yes."

Charlie glanced at other men who said nothing. He began to read through the document. The non-disclosure was written with great care. On the last page, in bold print, it stated that Charlie would be subject to a $250 thousand penalty if he disclosed a word to anyone about the nature of this meeting. He signed the document and handed it to Max.

"Charlie, we're looking at some real estate, and we want you to negotiate the deal."

"What? I took the redeye from Acapulco to talk about real estate?"

"This is no ordinary real estate transaction. It's five hundred thousand square miles of land."

Charlie did a quick calculation. "If sixth grade geography serves me right, Texas only has two hundred fifty thousand square miles of land. So, if you're talking about a piece of land twice that size, I'll assume it's not in the U.S?"

"You're right. It's in Canada. We want to buy Manitoba and Saskatchewan."

Charlie was dumbfounded. What Max just said made no sense. He looked at the other men in the room. They remained stone-faced and quiet. "I'm not following. Why would you want those provinces?"

Max glanced at the other men and then back at Charlie. "Let's just say we're interested in making a long-term investment."

"Let me ask my question another way. Why would Canada sell a bunch of investors a large chunk of their country? Especially two provinces with oil and natural gas fields. That alone is worth a fortune."

"They keep all the oil and gas that's in the ground. And if, somehow, a diamond mine is discovered, they can keep that, too, along with all other natural resources."

Charlie leaned back in his chair and placed his hands behind his head. "Nothing you're saying makes sense to me, Max. This is the most bizarre meeting I've ever attended." He waited for Max to level with him, and after a moment more of silence he knew it wasn't going to happen. "We both know you're not telling me everything."

"Well, I'll tell you this. We're prepared to pay you $5 million to negotiate the deal for us. If you succeed, you'll receive another $10 million when the deal's consummated."

"Why not get Trump? He's *forgotten* more about real estate than I'll ever begin to know."

"Trump would be a good choice. But, for reasons I can't divulge, the committee wants you. Are you interested?"

Charlie folded his hands on the table. It is rare in life when you are guaranteed a huge sum of money whether you succeed or not. On the other hand, Max was not telling him everything.

"Bring a team onboard if you want, as long as they play by the rules. That means we vet each team member, and, if they're approved, they sign our non-disclosure. Is that clear?"

"It's clear, but I'll need to think this over. Is there a deadline to get back to you?"

"ASAP, Charlie. We need to get started in the next day or two."

"How much are you willing to pay for the land?"

"We're working those numbers now. I'll know in a couple of days, and that's when I'll expect to hear back from you."

Max stood and Charlie knew the meeting was over. The two men shook hands, and as Charlie walked from the room, he glanced at the men sitting around the table. They watched him leave, but no one spoke a word. In the elevator ride down it occurred to him that he should have asked more questions. But the meeting was peculiar and had knocked him off his game. Charlie was sure of one thing. Something odd, maybe even bizarre, was going down; no one buys five hundred thousand square miles of land as a mere investment. He was also curious as to why they were willing to pay him $5 million for failing and another $10 million if he got lucky, especially knowing Canada would be insane to sell off any portion of their country, no matter what they were offered. Why would any country consider it?

CHAPTER FOUR

Angela stepped out into the street in front of her apartment building in Tribeca. She had sublet a place from a friend who was on tour in Europe for three months. She flagged a taxi and was dropped off in Times Square. She slipped on a pair of dark sunglasses so as not to be recognized as Senator Connolly's wife, and then walked to the end of the audition line that stretched down West 45th Street. It was the third cattle call she had attended this week. Her hopes were to fare much better this time than she had in the other auditions she'd graced with her singing. This audition was for a new show going into rehearsals, and more than anything she wanted to become part of the cast. It was called *Once Upon A Time* and the musical score consisted of blues, jazz, and pop from the Sixties through the Nineties. The music suited her sweet spot as she had grown up singing much of this music.

Angela pulled out the sheet music to "I Will Always Love You," the song made famous by Whitney Houston. Angela had the vocals to pull it off. With only one chance to impress at an audition, she was determined to match Whitney note for note.

Angela's cell phone vibrated. When she looked, she saw it was Charlie calling. To talk to him now might affect not only her emotions but also the quality of her audition, so she let his call go to voicemail. The line grew smaller. Ninety minutes later she was inside the theatre with only a handful of vocalists ahead of her. For the first time she was able to hear the talent level of other singers, and it was off the charts. It had been a while since she last performed in front of a group of people and for a moment her confidence waned. In addition to looking for the best vocal talent, the director was also searching for someone with the right look, tone, and personality to make the story believable.

"Angela. Please step to the center of the stage."

CHAPTER FIVE

Charlie had two top aides that he'd depended upon during his tenure in the Senate: Robert Devins and Delsi Kimberly. He decided that, if he agreed to approach the Canadian government with an offer to purchase two of their provinces, he wanted Robert and Delsi by his side. Both were bright, aggressive and got things done. The bad news was that they disagreed on practically everything. To have two aides whose philosophies reside at the opposite ends of the spectrum can be challenging, but Charlie drew from their strengths, their unabashed opinions, and their doggedness on issues that ranged from entitlements, deficit spending, and support for the best policies to improve the lives of Americans. Their combined efforts anchored him, and influenced the majority of the decisions he had made as senator.

Charlie had leased office space in the Chrysler Building when he returned to New York. He was sitting in the conference room when Robert entered.

"Thanks for dumping me in Acapulco. I wake up the next morning and you're gone."

"If I recall, you were out on the town the night before. You didn't miss me at all."

"Well, I didn't expect to be abandoned, that's all."

"When Delsi gets here, I'll explain my reason for leaving so suddenly. And if Delsi's in a bad mood, don't antagonize her. But, if you decide to ignore my advice, please wait until I've said my piece."

A smile came to Robert's face. Charlie depended on him to remain calm and collected when things heated up. He counted on Robert to suggest a solution that benefited everyone, something he succeeded at most of the time. The only person to consistently rile him was Delsi.

There was a tap on the door. Delsi Kimberly stuck her head into the conference room. She flashed a smile and entered. She wore a navy blue suit and white shirt open at the collar. Her blonde hair was a cross between shaggy and stringy, and appeared unkempt. When she stepped closer, however, your attention was drawn to her eyes, two large pools that pulled you in and held you captive. When challenged for any reason, her face would tighten and her eyes pierced right through you, throwing you off balance. The distraction had caused Robert to lose more than a few heated debates to her. Then, in a brief moment her eyes were soft again, and her face glimmered in the most striking way. While some found these qualities attractive, others found them seductive. One thing was certain: no one ever considered Delsi boring. Even her name was a portmanteau of the first names of her parents: Delores and Silas, now both passed on.

As a child, Delsi found more enjoyment watching a praying mantis stalk a cricket than she did playing with dolls. She once became friends with another girl in middle school, but she exhausted the poor girl with so much political trivia, theories on the expanding universe, and what the future of mankind would have in store for us, that the girl stopped playing with her. By the time Delsi was a sophomore in high school, she had read most of the books written by the great writers and thinkers. At age fifteen she had developed a soft spot for Genghis Khan. At M.I.T. she majored in Economics. Of course it was no surprise that her conservative politics clashed with the ideologies of her mostly liberal professors and classmates. After graduation, Delsi taught as an assistant professor at numerous schools. But over the years, the glamour of correcting papers and giving tests had worn itself out. By chance, she had met Senator Charlie Connolly. He was looking for an aide that understood economics, the politics of Washington, congressional budgets, and who could assist him with writing impressive and influential documents.

Charlie got up and kissed her on the cheek. "Thanks for coming."

She threw her coat and bag on the table and sat down. "How could I not come, Charlie? You were so mysterious on the phone."

"Let me tell you what's going on." Charlie pulled out the non-disclosure agreement. "First, read this over and sign it."

They scanned the twenty pages "Are you joking? A $250 thousand fine if I divulge any information?" Robert said.

Charlie did not answer. He waited for them to read the document in its entirety. Without further comments, they both signed it and slid it across the table to him. "All right, I met with Max Plummer two days ago and he's asked me to negotiate a real estate deal for him and a group of his investors. The deal is kind of peculiar for a couple of reasons. First, they're willing to pay me a rather large sum, even if the deal falls through. If I'm successful, they'll triple the sum."

"Sounds like Max is throwing you a bone. You are out of work, but on the other hand, you're no real estate expert either," Robert said.

"Another thing, I'm not sure why they selected me. When I asked why they didn't reach out to Trump, they never gave me a straight answer. All they said was they wanted me to handle the negotiations, which brings me to an even stranger point: They want to purchase Manitoba and Saskatchewan."

"As in Canada?" Delsi said.

"You got it."

Delsi and Robert looked at each other. They looked as confused as Charlie had been when Max told him the same thing.

"It appears something's going on. Something unusual," Delsi said. "How much are they willing to pay for the land?"

"I'm not sure, but I'll find out tomorrow if I agree to negotiate this deal."

"Why are you having a problem with this?" Robert said.

"The way this deal is unfolding seems a little weird. I might regret getting involved."

"Your instincts are good, Charlie," Delsi said. "Here's what I propose. Schedule the meeting, and take Robert and me with you. We'll ask direct questions and expect direct answers. If Max refuses to disclose the information we request, then simply tell him you're not interested."

"Hold on," Robert said. "How much they paying you?"

Charlie hesitated for a moment. "Five million, and if the deal goes through, they'll add another ten million to it."

"What about us?"

"Four hundred thousand each. And if we close the deal, you each receive $1.2 million."

"And why are you not interested in this deal?" Robert said. "I would think—

"Just as I always suspected," Delsi said, cutting him off. "The greedy liberal finally shows his true colors." She looked over at Charlie. "Tell Max and his gang that you won't get involved in any under-the-table deals. Oh, and if you don't get the warm and fuzzies during this meeting, tell Max to find himself another boy."

"So, you're back to name calling already? All I asked Charlie was why he's hesitating with so much money on the table. I never said take the money and run. Nor did I suggest that Charlie act in any unethical manner. And I'm surprised that a capitalist p–"

"Hold on, you two. Before you start ripping skin off bones, let's stay on track. I need to know that if I agree to this deal you're both willing to come on board with me."

"Count me in," Robert said.

"I'm with you as long as this project is above board," Delsi said.

"Okay. With you two on board, I have some sense of comfort." Charlie looked at them. "You now have my permission to attack each other."

Robert looked at Delsi and a small smile crept onto his face. It had been a while since they last debated. Although he felt an urge to twist her into knots, he resisted. "There'll be no attack from me," Robert said. "The election is over and the president will remain in office. He was not booted onto Pennsylvania Avenue, or disgraced. Nor was he run out of Washington on a rail, as Delsi so eloquently predicted."

"Yes, Backer O'Boyle will remain in office for another term, but historians will point to his reelection as a low point in American history. Here's a man who had two objectives when he was first elected: to ram O'Boyle-care down our throats, and to campaign for reelection. Rather than work to create jobs, he schmoozed with the glitterati to the tune of two hundred fifteen fundraisers, a Guinness Book record no doubt. And, of course fundraising can be tiring, so he relaxed by getting in one hundred fifteen rounds of golf, not counting vacations. So let me see if I've got this right: Unemployment is at a record high; the country's debt is growing by $4 billion a day; he's broken every campaign promise he made; and while he's out yelling 'Fore' on some golf course, another twenty-two million Americans have been placed on the dole to collect welfare and food stamps. How is it possible this guy was reelected?"

"Well, let me address your point about food stamps. Being a righteous capitalist, you would rather see millions of people thrown into the streets and their children starve," Robert said.

"I would rather have a president who thinks it's important to create jobs for those millions of people. But it requires having a clue on how to create them."

"He's a much better choice than Matt Roman, a man who despises the poor. Is there any wonder why forty-seven percent didn't vote for him? His kind only cares about making the wealthy wealthier. And, don't forget, it's taken Backer O'Boyle four years to pry the economy out from under the damage done by McBush. Just watch, he'll turn this country around in ways you won't believe."

"That's my biggest fear." Delsi threw her hands up. "You know what? I'm done talking about this. Your president won. You have the right to your gloat tour, and I only have two things to say. First, you haven't changed, Robert. You're still an idiot. And second, Ralph Bunche."

"Ralph Bunche?"

"Look him up. You'll learn something important about what it means to be an American."

"All right," Charlie said. "Sounds like this debate has reached its end, so let's change the subject and get down to business. I want to outline everything we're going to say to Max Plummer when we meet with him tomorrow."

CHAPTER SIX

Kaitlin took out her new cell phone to explore the features it offered. Her parents had given her the phone to maintain access with her when she was away from home. She was not to use the phone to call her friends. As she stepped off her school bus the phone rang. "Hi, Daddy."

"How are you, Sweetheart?"

"I'm walking into school. Are you coming to see me soon?"

"That's why I'm calling. I want to come, but I haven't heard back from your mother. I've left her a couple of messages."

"She's been pretty busy, Daddy. She auditioned for a Broadway show last week and they called her back for a second audition."

"That's great. Will you ask her to call me?"

"I will, Daddy. Are you coming to the picnic on Sunday? The whole family will be there."

"It's this weekend? I'm glad you reminded me. Tell your mother to call me. And don't worry, I'll be at the picnic."

"I can't wait to see you."

"I can't wait either, Sweetheart. I want to hear everything you've been doing. I love you, Kaitlin."

"I love you too, Daddy."

* * *

Max Plummer sat at the head of the table with five other men seated alongside him. "Sit anywhere you like, Charlie."

Max introduced the other men; they were all CEOs from some of the largest corporations in the United States. Charlie had forwarded Robert and Delsi's personal information to Max. Both were vetted and given clearance to attend the meeting.

"You've decided to take the position?"

"Not yet, Max. First, tell us what's really going down."

Max looked at the other men. One of them nodded to him. "Well, Charlie, we were hoping the money would entice you not to ask too many questions, but I see that's not the case. Let me start here. As you know, companies are leaving the U.S. in droves and setting up off-shore operations, mostly to save tens of millions of dollars in corporate taxes. Amazon, Google, and Starbucks, just to name a few, are saving hundreds of millions. Well, six months ago we were contacted by a party who laid out a very interesting proposal. He said that, instead of each individual corporation setting up their own off-shore operation, we should be more enterprising—pursue a more dynamic approach where we never find ourselves at the mercy of another country. In short, he suggested that we purchase Manitoba and Saskatchewan."

"Just like that, right out of the blue?"

"It sounded humorous at first. But this man convinced us—and I'm talking about the heads of every Fortune 500—to meet with him. When we did, he delivered a presentation that took us by surprise. Here we were, thinking he was some kind of tax accountant. But instead, he explained some events that are going to occur in the United States over the next decade, and that saving corporate taxes was the least of our concern. To not heed his advice, he pointed out, and to stay in the U.S., would bring financial losses to our companies in the trillions, and many would face ruin."

"You tell a great story, Max, but when I walked in here, I asked you to level with me. You can't possibly expect us to believe a cornball story like that? Now, if you told me that corporations have come up with a scheme to leverage the government into relaxing some of the hard-ass regulations you guys recently had to swallow, I could believe that. I could even believe you're going to pressure the government into shaving down some of those tax increases that are expected to pass legislation next month. But don't tell me a fairy tale."

"I'm afraid you're wrong, Charlie. Everything I've told you is the absolute truth."

"You're telling me some person assembled CEOs from all five hundred companies, and in one meeting convinced some of the smartest men in the world to leave the U.S.?"

Max looked at the other CEOs and then back at Charlie. "That's pretty much what I'm telling you. It was the most compelling presentation I've ever sat through. There were three core elements to it. It was information we had all heard before, and I know this sounds crazy, but when we heard this person say it, it took on a whole new meaning. He even made predictions about what would occur if O'Boyle was reelected. So, we all waited to see if his predictions were true, and every single one has occurred exactly as he said it would. Understand, what we are about to embark upon, to leave this country, is not something we take lightly. All the information has been compiled and analyzed, but it all came down to this one person whose insight sealed our decision to leave."

"How many companies are leaving?"

"I can't divulge that to anyone unless they're on board with us."

"Did Canada contact you?"

"No one else has approached us, only this one individual."

"Who?"

Max looked at the other men and got their support. "His name is Michael Reny."

"Michael Reny? I've heard his name before, but I thought he was dead. I remember an article about Reny helping Argentina with their currency. He stabilized their economy."

"I'd heard stories, too," Max said. "He worked in the copper mines of Chile and helped improve conditions for the miners there, but I haven't heard his name mentioned in years."

One of the men at the table cleared his throat and Charlie looked over at him. It was the first time a CEO other than Max spoke. "He worked as a laborer on the Brazilian railroad, too." The CEO said. "He spoke fluent Portuguese when telling stories to the workers there, so we assumed he was Brazilian. Then, in the middle of the labor strike, he just up and vanished.

Someone said they saw him hook on with a freighter in São Vicente, and after that he was never seen again."

"I'd heard about Michael Reny from a friend of mine in South Africa," another CEO said. "Reny led the workers' protest against low wages in the diamond mines. And, one day in the middle of the uprising, he just disappeared."

"All interesting stories," Charlie said. "But Max, why did you pick me to negotiate with the Canadian government?"

"I didn't pick you, Charlie. Michael Reny did."

It was a rare moment for Delsi and Robert to see a look of surprise come across Charlie's face.

"I don't even know the man."

"Well, when we sat down to figure out who should spearhead this project, a lot of names were thrown out, but Reny was adamant that you should be the one."

Charlie turned to Robert and Delsi for help.

"I think I speak for Charlie when I say we need to meet this Michael Reny and hear his presentation," Delsi said. "Once we understand it, Charlie will give his answer. Can you arrange a meeting, Max?"

"I don't know if he'll meet with you. We've met with Reny only once. He's the shy type, and not real fond of publicity or meeting with people. He likes to stay in the background."

"I see," Robert said. "He has no problem creating a revolution, as long as he does his disappearing act before everything blows up."

"Max, you've put me in a tough spot," Charlie said. "There are questions you can't answer, and the only person who can doesn't like the company of people. I'd call that a real dilemma. So, let me be clear with you: Either we meet with this Reny character and hear his presentation, or I have no choice but to walk."

"You don't leave me much choice, do you," Max said. "All right, I'll contact him. It'll be interesting to see what he says."

"We'll wait to hear back from you, Max."

Charlie, Robert and Delsi walked to the door. Before leaving, Charlie turned to Max and asked, "Did you ever decide on a price for the land?"

"We did. When you come aboard I'll share that number with you."

CHAPTER SEVEN

The picnic area at Flushing Meadows Park has an abundance of tables, barbecue pits, and wide open spaces for kids to run and play. It was where the Robinson family had been convening once a year ever since Angela was a child, and the one event her mother, brothers, cousins, aunts and uncles never missed.

Angela arrived early with Kaitlin to secure as many tables and barbecue pits as possible for the sixty family members who would arrive over the next two hours.

"Hey, Sister."

Angela turned around. "Marcus." She opened her arms and embraced her big brother, whom she hadn't seen in months. She then grabbed hold of the love handle hanging over his belt. "You gettin' real healthy, boy."

Marcus laughed. "That's home cookin' for ya." He looked over his shoulder. "Here comes the culprit now."

Angela pulled her brother's wife Charisa into a three-way hug. "Girl, you looking good."

"And you still lookin' like a movie star. Let me put this bag down, I've got another one to lug from the car." She looked at Marcus. Getting the hint, he headed to the car.

There were hugs, kisses and high fives as more members of the Robinson family arrived. The men got busy filling the barbecue pits with charcoal while the women prepared chicken, pork ribs, hot dogs and hamburgers. Young boys were scattered on the grass throwing footballs and baseballs. Others ran off to play a two-on-two game on the basketball court. Some of the girls stayed with their moms to help prepare the food, while others showed off their new jeans and cell phones, and talked about the cute boys at school. The picnic would last late into the day, and end with their annual family softball game.

Charlie arrived an hour later than Angela. He walked into the park and saw Kaitlin in the distance. He quickened his pace until he got within earshot. "Hello, Sweetheart."

Kaitlin turned around when she heard his voice. She ran and jumped into his arms, clutching him without saying a word. Charlie saw Angela near the tables and, with Kaitlin in his arms, walked in her direction. Angela saw him approach. She ran over and hugged them both. Charlie leaned over and kissed her on the lips. "I've missed you." A tear rolled down her cheek and she buried her face in his chest. The extended family kept busy with preparations and talking to each other, but they could not resist eying Charlie and Angela. It was heartening to see them together again.

Kaitlin pulled away from Charlie. "I'm going to visit with my cousins now, Daddy. You and Mommy talk, okay?"

"Okay, Honey." He let her down and she ran off in the direction of a bunch of girls who were giggling and laughing. Charlie put his arm around Angela and they strolled off in the opposite direction. "I heard you've been asked back for a second audition."

"I told Kaitlin not to say anything. I haven't mentioned it to my family yet, and I won't unless I'm lucky enough to get the part. I don't want to get my hopes too high."

"It's a musical?"

"Yes. It's called *Once Upon A Time*. It's a story told with music, and it's about America from the Fifties until now. The music speaks to the beauty of our country, how some of that beauty is now gone, and how the world has changed over the years."

"When will they make their final decision?"

"This coming week. It's down to three of us, and we're all pretty good," Angela said. "If I don't mind saying so myself."

Charlie smiled. "You'll get the part. And when you do, we'll celebrate."

Angela stopped. A look of concern came over her face. "I need more time, Charlie. I need to find myself again."

Charlie turned to face her. "I'm sorry I haven't done better. You deserve much more from me."

Angela laid her head on his chest and he wrapped his arms around her.

Kaitlin tracked them down. "Hey, Daddy, watch this." She dipped a large, round wand into a container of fluid and then blew on it. A bubble the size of a basketball appeared. It floated in the air and caught the attention of other kids. Kaitlin blew another bubble the same size, and within moments she was encircled by a dozen of her cousins. "Let me do it. Let me try it," they yelled. Kaitlin handed the wand to one of her cousins, and they ran off. Charlie and Angela walked back to the table.

Angela began to pull food out of a bag and Charlie lit the charcoals. Afterwards, he went from table to table to greet the other Robinsons. Shaking so many hands reminded him of being on the campaign trail. When he returned to their table, Angela was putting ribs on the barbecue. He sat down on the bench and idly began to whistle "America the Beautiful" while looking up toward the trees, at nothing in particular.

One of Angela's cousins at the next table observed Charlie and began to chuckle. Charlie did not hear him as he daydreamed and continued whistling. Before long, he had caught the attention of other Robinsons who also began to chuckle at him. Angela turned around to see what all the fuss was about, only to see Charlie, still gazing up at the trees, whistling away, oblivious to those watching him and enjoying a good laugh at his expense.

"Charlie!" Angela yelled.

Charlie stopped and looked at her.

"Quit that! You're embarrassing yourself."

He looked around and realized he was the center of attention. He stopped whistling. The Robinson family continued to laugh, however, and he, too, began to laugh. Soon Angela began to laugh when she saw her brother Marcus bent over in laughter and grabbing his sides. She sat down next to Charlie. The silly expression on his face made her double over in laughter as well. She tried to say something to Charlie, but every time she tried to speak, she burst into laughter once again. Finally she managed to say it. "Do you know how embarrassing it is to hear you whistle that tune? Can't you whistle some Al Green?"

With that, Charlie buckled over and let out a belly laugh, which caused everyone else to laugh even harder. After a minute, the laughter died down. But then Charlie made the mistake of looking at Angela, and it began all over again. This time Angela fell on her knees next to the bench, and Charlie, already weak from laughter, tried to lift her up, but it was not to happen. They fumbled over each other which drove the family into a laughing jag.

"You know what?" Charlie managed to say.

"What?" Angela said.

"Why don't *you* sing "America the Beautiful?"

"I'll sing it, all right. At your funeral!" Tears ran down her face and she grabbed her sides and fell on the grass. Charlie collapsed on top of her and hadn't the strength to get up. The family encircled them and everyone was growing weak from laughter. Other people in the park wondered what could possibly be going on, because every minute or so a roar of laughter erupted.

Kaitlin returned from playing with her cousins and found her parents lying on the grass laughing. She bent down and hugged them both, then looked up at the rest of the family with an appreciative smile. It took five minutes before things returned to normal. Slowly the family disbanded and returned to their tables and barbecue pits. Charlie and Angela found the strength to lift themselves off the ground. Angela returned to oversee the chicken and ribs on the barbecue pit and Charlie remained on the bench with Kaitlin on his lap.

Angela looked over her shoulder. "Tell your daddy what you memorized, and who it's from."

"We have to memorize a speech and say it in front of the class next week. Mommy picked one from Dr. Martin Luther King." Kaitlin became self-conscious and buried her head in Charlie's chest.

"Don't be shy. Recite it for me."

"Okay. Here's the part I memorized: 'I don't know what will happen now. We've got some difficult days ahead. But it doesn't matter with me now. Because I've been to the mountaintop. I don't mind. Like anybody, I would like to live a long life. But I'm not concerned about that now. I just want to do God's will. And He's allowed me to go to the mountain. And I've looked over. And I've seen the Promised Land. I may not get there with you. But I want you to know tonight, that we, as people, will get to the Promised Land. So I'm happy tonight. I'm not worried about anything. I'm not fearing any man. Mine eyes have seen the glory of the coming of the Lord.'"

Charlie sat in silence for a moment. "You said that beautifully, Kaitlin. Do you know what happened to Dr. King on the following day?"

"Mommy said a bad man killed him. He's in heaven now watching over us."

"That's right. And do you know what Dr. King expects from you?"

"Yes. I need to go to school and learn. I need to do my homework. And if I do that, when I grow up I will help America be the best country in the world."

Charlie pulled her close and hugged her. "I'm very proud of you, Honey."

"Tell your daddy what else happened in school."

"Some people want us to stop saying the 'Pledge of Allegiance.' They don't want God mentioned in school anymore."

"When did this happen?"

"Last week, Daddy."

"I heard they've been doing this in a lot of school systems, and it's not right. I'm going to your school tomorrow. I want to speak with your principal about it."

"Are you going to take me to school in the morning, Daddy?"

Charlie looked at Angela. "If your mother doesn't mind me coming by to pick you up."

Angela looked over her shoulder at him. "You can come by and take her."

Charlie held Angela's gaze until she smiled at him.

"Good, it's settled then."

CHAPTER EIGHT

The call came from Max Plummer. Michael Reny had agreed to meet with Charlie and his team. There were conditions, though. Since Reny's schedule did not allow him much time, the presentation needed to be delivered over a three-day period. The time and place would also be decided by Reny.

At eight o'clock the next morning Charlie and his team arrived to the disclosed location on Varick Street. It was a five-story non-descript building in the middle of the block. When they stepped off the elevator onto the fifth floor, they walked down the barely lit hallway and into a small conference room. The lights were off in the room. Standing in front of the window with his back to them was a tall, lean, silhouetted man. He quietly turned to face them, with only the outline of his head and neck visible. Slowly, he made his way across the room until he stood in front of them, and only then did they glimpse the outline of his face.

Two large, sagacious eyes peered down at them. "I'm Michael Reny." A hand appeared. Charlie took it first, and then Robert. Delsi lifted her hand to feel Reny's fingers like warm tentacles wrap around her hand and part of her wrist. His touch was distinctly different in feel from any she had ever come in contact with before. When she looked into his eyes she saw kindness and intelligence. Even in the darkened room, light radiated from them. He explored her face and gave the feeling he could will her to offer up her deepest secrets.

Reny let go of her hand. He walked to the wall and turned on the lights. "I apologize. Darkness relaxes me. Please, have a seat." Charlie, Robert and Delsi all sat while Reny took the seat across the table from them. In the lighted room everyone saw his face more clearly. He had rugged features and a two-inch scar down the side of one cheek. His dark brown hair was neatly combed to one side, and, as his three guests continued to study him, Reny looked across at them, grinning modestly. If they didn't know better, they'd consider him shy.

Reny sat erect with a great deal of assurance and folded his hands on the table in front of him. Charlie tried to determine his age, but he was unable to do so.

"I was surprised when Max said you wanted me for this project."

"You were my first choice."

"Can you tell me why?"

Reny's intense look made Charlie feel he was the only person in the world.

"I've followed your career and I admire the way you conduct yourself."

Charlie raised his eyebrows. "Maybe you didn't see the results of my last election."

Reny smiled. "You showed great character throughout the campaign. Your opponent was a blemished man, and to publicly disgrace him on any number of issues was well within your reach. You chose not to run that kind of campaign. The election was lost, Charlie, but your character remains intact." Reny looked at his watch. "Max explained to you my schedule problem, I'm sure. I'll need to leave soon."

"What about your presentation?"

"It was never my intent to present today. I wanted us to meet first. Our meeting will occur soon."

"Is it possible to give your presentation in one meeting?" Charlie looked over at Robert and Delsi, and back to Reny. "These are two very bright people who digest information with a high degree of alacrity. We'll get the picture fairly quickly."

"I have no doubt. But only one presentation was given to the Fortune 500. That one lasted three hours; an amount of time I cannot afford to spend in any one day with you. I must break my presentation to you into three sessions. Please trust that my presentation will be offered in the most effective way."

"Fair enough. How do I contact you?"

Reny stood up. "No need. I'll notify you."

They had arrived only minutes earlier, and the meeting was already over. Charlie stood up and shook hands with Reny. As they left the room, Reny called out to him.

"Charlie, the answer to the question you did not ask is: Ralph Bunche."

CHAPTER NINE

(ONE WEEK BEFORE THE PRESIDENTIAL ELECTION)

The alarm rang at six a.m. Delilah Jones reached over without looking and shut it off. She lay there a minute longer before rolling her feet onto the floor and standing up.

"Come on, Ronnie. Get up."

Ronnie stretched his arms and legs before rolling over and dozing off again. Delilah walked to the outer room where her mother Mabel was asleep on the couch.

"Come on Mama. It's another day."

"You votin'?"

"Not today, mama. I'll try an' git down there beforehand, or just go election day." Delilah walked into the small kitchen and turned on the hot plate to cook Ronnie's oatmeal. "Ronnie," she yelled. "Git out of that bed and git dressed for school." The kitchen stove hadn't worked for months, even though the landlord had promised to fix it. "Ronnie, I'm not tellin' you again. Come git these oats." Mabel got up and walked into the bathroom to change out of her nightgown and into her dress. After washing her face and hands, she returned to the couch to fold the blanket and place the pillow on the back of the couch to give Ronnie room to eat his breakfast.

"Ronnie, if I come in–"

"I'm up, Mom." Ronnie walked out of the bedroom and sat on the couch as Delilah carried his hot oats into the room and placed them on the coffee table and walked away. He rubbed his eyes for a moment and looked at the floor, as though he were in a daze.

"I want those oats eaten' before I leave for the bus stop," Delilah yelled as she washed up and dressed in the bathroom.

"Mom?"

"What?"

"I need new sneakers. Mine have a hole in 'em."

"Well, put some cardboard in 'em for now. I'll go by the outlet on my way home."

"Mom?"

"Now what?"

"Can I get Air Jordans?"

Delilah walked into the outer room and stared at him. "I ain't spendin' no hundred twenty dollars to put Jordon rubber under your feet. Not when you can git 'em for twenty-eight."

"Freddie's mom is getting' em for him. Lots of kids at school got 'em. All I ever wear is outlet stuff."

Delilah slipped on a sweater and buttoned it over her buxom chest. As she walked to the door she said, "There mo' important things in this world than Jordans. You gettin' As and Bs in school is one. Now eat those oats before I go."

Ronnie stuck a spoonful in his mouth and chewed before swallowing them down. Delilah waited until his bowl was empty. "Come here."

Ronnie walked over to his mother. Delilah cupped her hands on his face. "You pay 'tention in school, and tonight tell me what you learned." She kissed him on the forehead and pulled him to her bosom. "Mama, stay with 'em 'til the school bus come, and be there when it drop him off."

"You tell me every day, Delilah. I know to watch 'em."

Delilah grabbed her purse and was out the door. She walked past the other row houses that look exactly like her own. She crossed the busy intersection and caught the bus for the hour and twenty minute ride across town to the Sunshine Supermarket, where she had been working as a grocery bagger for nine months. She makes extra money cleaning in the back room and breaking down cardboard boxes when they get stacked too high. She gets paid ten dollars an hour and is one of the lucky ones who works forty hours a week, which qualifies for Sunshine's health insurance. Delilah was grateful for this, having a young son at home.

After work, Delilah rode the bus back home, arriving at seven thirty. She checked Ronnie's homework and talked about the meaning of college once again. Ronnie was in bed by nine o'clock, and Delilah read to him. After finishing the story she rubbed Ronnie's back, humming softly until he fell asleep. Then she pulled her sweater over her shoulders and left for her second job, cleaning an office building. To get there she took the bus back across town. She arrived at ten thirty and cleaned until one thirty in the morning. The last bus of the night got her back home an hour later. She tiptoed past her mama on the couch and into the bedroom.

The alarm rang at six a.m. Delilah reached over and shut it off. She lay there a minute longer before rolling her feet onto the floor and standing up.

"Come on, Ronnie. Get up for school."

Chapter Ten

It was a challenge to sleep after meeting Michael Reny. What could he possibly have told the Fortune 500 CEOs to convince them to leave the U.S., and just how many companies did he actually convince? Delsi got out of bed and powered up her computer. Within an hour she had created a mathematical model of what the U.S. economy would look like if one hundred of these companies were to leave. She then plugged two hundred companies into her model, and then three hundred. By six a.m. Delsi fully understood the devastation these companies would leave in their wake.

Delsi looked up at the window and saw it was light outside. Her eyes were tired, but this was not the time to sleep. She got dressed and went to the office. Charlie and Robert would be in by seven, and as the moments ticked away, Michael Reny invaded her mind. Her thoughts went to his expressive eyes, and how they made her feel the moment he first looked at her. And his touch—never had the touch of anyone's hand made her heart race. Just one brief encounter with this man had given rise to unfamiliar yet exciting feelings.

"Delsi. You're in early." Robert took a seat across the table from her.

"Morning."

"Hey, about the other day. I hope you didn't think I was gloating about O'Boyle's re-election. I never meant to insult you. I was just having fun."

"You didn't insult me, and I'm not angry. It's just that something's changed in this country and O'Boyle's re-election is an omen. I can't put my finger on it, but I feel like we're on a ship adrift at sea without a rudder and no one seems to care. I always believed that people would make the choice that was best for the country, but it just didn't happen."

"What are you referring to?"

"Look, Robert, I don't want to rehash it. Your guy got elected, and you and millions of other people are happy about that. But things occurred in this election that should have repulsed every person in this country, and they didn't. I have to question who we are as citizens. Regardless of party, I would disown my candidate if he had no accomplishments to run on and spent $2 billion for the sole purpose of defaming his opponent. That money could have been used for so many important programs, but O'Boyle spent it to make Matt Roman look bad. I'm not even angry with O'Boyle as much as I am with the people of this country. O'Boyle's a politician; he'll do whatever he can to get elected. But why weren't we smart enough to see through him? His only chance to win was to make his opponent look worse than him."

"Umm, could it be that making Matt Roman look bad was fairly easy to do? Could it be that Roman scared the hell out of every minority in the country? Not to mention that most women found it hard to sleep at night."

"Robert, that's what I'm talking about, the brainwashing crap. O'Boyle told a clever story and America swallowed it. Roman is a man who has never taken a drink or smoked a cigarette in his life. He's a great husband and a loving father, and more importantly, he knows how to create jobs, exactly what this country needs. And yet, the voters, many of them unemployed, picked the guy who couldn't create a job if his life depended upon it. Too many Americans no longer think about what's best for the country."

"Matt Roman is a corporate pig and doesn't care one iota about the poor that go hungry in this country. The best man got elected."

"I thought we were having an intelligent conversation, and you go and say something like that. You know what Robert? You're an idiot."

Robert regretted making the statement, but on the other hand, it had been a while since fire shot from Delsi's eyes. He loved her odd, combustible nature, and her reaction to him was pleasing because no one displayed anger as magnificently as Delsi. He thought back to one occasion in particular, after one of their knock-down drag-out debates a year ago. He could not recall who won the debate that day, but afterwards he had asked her to dinner. To his surprise she accepted. He made reservations at The Four Seasons to impress her, but an hour past their agreed-upon meeting time she was a no-show. Thirty minutes later he ordered off the menu and ate dinner alone. The next morning when Robert asked her what had happened, Delsi said she got tied up in a project and lost track of the time. She said it matter-of-factly, which was just like her. No apology, no emotion, no sense of guilt or that she might have inconvenienced him. Yet, Robert still found himself attracted to her.

"Sorry I'm late." Charlie said, walking into the room and tossing his briefcase down. "Good news, though. Michael Reny called and scheduled time to meet with us."

"Can't wait," Robert said. "What could he possibly tell us?"

"We'll find out soon enough. So, what's on today's agenda?"

"Robert and I just concluded an all-embracing far-reaching chat. He was so illuminating that I forgot to mention the model I created last night. Now that Michael Reny has scheduled time for us, it may serve us well to be forearmed before going into that meeting."

"Very well said. The floor is all yours."

"I've put together a mathematical model on, for lack of a better phrase, the tipping point that will induce this country to implode. The model shows the country's condition if two hundred and fifty Fortune 500 companies were to pack up and leave for Canada. First, let's look at the mass exodus scenario where the government is caught flat-footed and unaware of their evacuation. Initial damage will be felt on Wall Street when the stock market plunges. To be perfectly candid, every stock listed will crash and burn, and make what occurred in 1929 look like a walk in the park. Mutual funds, retirement funds, investment funds, you name it, they'll all be devastated and their return to full value would be quite doubtful.

"Now, run this model the same way, with the two hundred and fifty corporations leaving, but where the U.S. government has been notified in advance that these companies are moving to Canada. In this scenario, where there's an orchestrated exit strategy, say, over a five-year period, in this case, the U.S can withstand the blow. The stock market would still be ravaged, but over time it would rebound, although never to its original value.

"Let's consider job loss, because these corporations may plan to move a mass of people to Canada. I scaled the number at five million. The tax loss created by losing these corporations would be bad enough, but when you take away tax revenue from five million productive workers, this country will be headed in a downward spiral. It's not a rosy picture.

"As I mentioned, the inevitable collapse occurs when two hundred and fifty corporations leave. Their departure will become the catalyst for hundreds of other corporations to leave as well, because if any one corporation stays, their stock will be worth nothing. We're looking at hundreds of billions, possibly trillions, of lost value, and many of these companies will fall into bankruptcy if they remain in the U.S.

"When these corporations leave, unemployment will reach the fifty percentile. Soon after, inflation will wreak havoc to the point where few people will be able to afford the cost of food. Mortgage payments will no longer be made, schools will shut down, and people will roam the streets looking for food. It hurts me to say these words, but everyday people from the ranks of the rich to the poor will pillage, plunder, and lay waste to most of our nation. The U.S. Army and National Guard can lock down only five percent of the country, mostly the larger cities. So, theft and even murder will run rampant in the outlying regions of the country. Finally, I can say with certainty the United States will cease to exist as we know it today."

Charlie and Robert remained frozen in their chairs, their eyes glued to Delsi. They waited for her to add *but...*, thinking perhaps her model had an escape route to prevent the sacking of the nation. They waited in silence for her to deliver that solution, but after another minute had passed, it became apparent that Delsi had said everything she had to say.

Charlie cleared his throat. "Reny can tell us whatever he wants in our meeting with him, but the Fortune 500 cannot leave. They need to stay and do what's right for America."

CHAPTER ELEVEN

Charlie was preparing for his meeting with Michael Reny when his cell phone vibrated. When he saw it was Angela, he dropped everything to answer it. "Hi."

"I wanted you to be the first to know. I got it!"

"Fantastic! You must be walking on air."

"I am. I feel so good."

"Let's have dinner tonight to celebrate."

"I can't. Rehearsal starts this afternoon and we'll be going six days a week until we open. Sunday's my only day off."

"Sunday then. We'll make it a family affair."

"Kaitlin would like that, and so would I."

"Let's do something special. How about we drive upstate and find a restaurant somewhere? That's always fun."

"Sounds charming. I have to go Charlie. They're calling me back into rehearsal."

"I love you, Angela."

"I love you, too."

* * *

(Twelve Years Earlier)

"Come on, Charlie. You'll like this place. They got music, and the bartender makes a helluva margarita."

Charlie deliberated outside the swanky restaurant. The two congressional aides frequented the place on a regular basis, mostly because it was packed tight with women. "All right, one drink and I'm out of here. I've got a report to complete."

"See, I told you we'd break him down." The aides laughed.

The bar area in the Post Restaurant was loud and wall to wall with people, many of whom were young women as promised. By six p.m. watering holes in the nation's seat were full. People went to meet old chums or co-workers, or, if they were lucky, new lovers. Charlie followed the two aides as they edged their way to the bar. The spot they chose was conveniently near two attractive, young women. One of the aides noticed the women needed their drinks refilled. He smiled and drew their attention. "My friend and I would love to buy you ladies a drink."

The women gave each aide the once-over. "That's very kind."

A conversation began and Charlie, only a few feet away, had no intention of butting in on his pals. From across the room he heard the tickle of piano keys and turned around. A young, woman with a striking appearance closed her eyes and began to sing "You Don't Know Me," a song he loved. Charlie had heard other renditions by the likes of Ray Charles, Kenny Rogers, Van Morrison, and Michael Bublé, but the way this woman sang made it sound brand new. Charlie could not take his eyes off of her. When she reached the bridge of the song, not another sound was heard at the bar. When she finished, enthusiastic applause erupted. Before she began her next song, she knew she had full command over the crowd. Charlie observed the faces of people watching her; he marveled at how her gift had captivated them. This young woman simply opened her mouth and the most natural, beautiful music filled the room.

After three more songs she took a break. She walked to the corner of the bar and asked for a glass of water. Charlie hesitated only a moment before walking to the end of the bar where she was standing. "Hello."

"Hello to you," she said with a smile.

"My name's Charlie."

"Nice to meet you, Charlie. I'm Angela."

"I just want to tell you how much I enjoy your music. I suppose you already know the effect you have on people."

Angela reached over and took her water from the bartender. She turned to face Charlie again. "I suppose. People tell me that."

"You have to be kidding. It's not every day I see a singer mesmerize a crowd the way you just did."

Angela sipped her water and smiled. "Are you a singer?"

"I whistle."

Angela almost choked on her water with laughter. "You're messing with me, right?"

"No, honestly, I whistle, mostly when I'm alone. Sometimes I whistle when I'm nervous, and other times when I'm feeling good. But rarely do I whistle in the company of other people."

Angela just looked at him. "I don't know if you're being serious or not, but you're very funny. Are you a comedian?"

"A comedian? I don't have a funny bone in my body."

Angela laughed again, briefly placing her hand on Charlie's chest as she composed herself. "You're very funny and you know it. Seriously, what do you do?"

Charlie shrugged. "I'm an aide."

Angela stared at him. "A nurse's aide?"

"No, a congressional aide. I work for Bob Miller. He's a state representative for New York. I do the grunt work and he gets all the credit. I'm here with two of my buddies." Charlie waved to his co-workers and they waved back. He looked at Angela again. "They come here a couple of times a week, but it's my first time here. Can I buy you a drink?"

"I don't drink."

"Can I get you something else?"

"Not really. One of the perks of working here is all the water I can drink."

"Want to sit down? Maybe we can talk a little."

"I'm starting my next set in a couple of minutes."

"Where are you from?"

"Brooklyn."

"You came all that way to perform here?"

"My agent booked me here."

"You came by yourself?"

"See that big guy standing over there watching you?"

Charlie turned to look. "Your boyfriend?"

"My brother Marcus. My family would never allow me to come to Washington by myself, so my brother drove me down."

"Sounds like your family cares a great deal about you."

"Yeah, we're close. I couldn't live away from my family. They're everything to me."

"Well, look, I'm going to be in New York City in two weeks. Would you like to go to dinner?"

Angela looked him over. "I'll have to think about that. You have those Casanova eyes, and my family is very protective when men come calling. And, if I did decide to go to dinner with you—and I'm not saying I will—my brother Marcus would insist on driving."

"Tell Marcus he can join us. As long as I get the chance to know you better."

Angela smiled. "Well, give me your card and we'll see what happens."

Charlie opened his wallet and handed her his card. "You know, this won't be easy for me. Every time the phone rings, I'm going to think it's you."

"Well, I have to get back to my piano."

"I'll wait for your call, Angela."

Five days later Charlie's cell phone rang. "Hi, Charlie. It's Angela."

CHAPTER TWELVE

Delilah stepped off the bus and walked five blocks to the shoe outlet on Gordon Street. It was Thursday and the store stayed open until ten p.m. Still, it didn't give her much time to buy Ronnie's sneakers and catch the next bus to her night job. There were not many size nine sneakers in the store, but she found a pair of blue and white Keds that had good rubber soles. She counted out twenty-two dollars and fifty-three cents and laid it on the counter. A minute later she was out the door walking back the five blocks to catch her bus. As Delilah was still a half a block from the bus stop, the bus whizzed by. She pulled out her schedule and saw she now had a forty-minute wait for the next bus to arrive. "Oh, no."

Delilah's office cleaning job was to vacuum the carpets, empty the trash cans and mop the hallway floors. Normally, she finished in time to catch the last bus home. Tonight, however, she missed the earlier bus, which meant she had to clean the building in record time in order to catch the last bus of the night.

She changed into her work clothes and took the elevator to the fourth floor. She found it easier to work from the top floor down. When she stepped off the elevator, she saw a note taped conspicuously on the wall in front of her. *Delilah, they held a going away party for an employee tonight. Please make sure their office is thoroughly cleaned. Thanks, Bill, Building Superintendent.* Delilah walked into the room and froze in her tracks. Countless half-filled plastic cups sat on desktops and paper plates with half-eaten food were strewn everywhere. Delilah knew that to clean the mess would take another hour of her time.

Two hours later Delilah was still cleaning the fourth floor. Every so often she looked up at the clock to see how she was doing on time, and it was not good. Then, reality set in: She realized she would not be on the last bus home tonight. She risked getting fired if she left without cleaning the entire building. She decided she would not go home tonight. And, when morning arrived, it made little sense to take the first bus home because she would have to get right back on the bus and travel across town to her supermarket job. She had prepared her mother if an event like this one occurred. *If I miss my bus, Mama, make sure Ronnie's up for school, feed him his oats, and stand with him 'til the bus comes.*

It was four a.m. by the time Delilah finished cleaning. She looked out the windows to see if there was an all-night diner nearby where she could get a cup of coffee, but the streets were dark and it frightened her to go out into the night alone. She also remembered her building swipe card was programmed to allow her in and out of the building only during certain hours, and if she left the building she would probably be locked out. She changed back into her street clothes and found a soft chair in one of the offices. A couple hours of sleep before leaving for her supermarket job was all she needed.

Delilah's mind drifted and she thought mostly about Ronnie. Why doesn't he eat more? What can she do to help him improve his B grades into A's? Her mind floated to Kenny. He had been her man, everything she had ever wanted. A good husband and father who, sadly, had changed over time, mostly because of the crowd he ran with in those days. It all came crashing down the night he was drunk and beat her. What hurt most was that he had done it in front of Ronnie. She can still see his little eyes filled with fear. Ronnie did not know the incidents of that night would change his world forever. The police came and Delilah pressed charges. Kenny was not allowed within five hundred feet of the house. Her eyes closed and her tired body got the rest it needed.

The morning light cascaded through the office window and woke Delilah. She pushed herself out of the chair and left the building. She caught the bus and arrived an hour before the supermarket opened, always observant of being on time for work and never giving anyone a reason to fire her. She worked the full day and took the bus home, arriving at her usual time. Mama told her that Ronnie had gotten off to school on time that morning, and that she had waited on the corner for the school bus to drop him off after school. Delilah sat next to Ronnie and watched him do his homework. When he was done she had him explain what the teacher had taught him at school that day. Ronnie pretended to be the teacher and excitedly began to explain the difference between latitude and longitude. A knock on the door interrupted them. Delilah and Mama looked at each other.

In their neighborhood, people didn't come knocking too often. But when they did, it was wise to look out the window to see who it was before opening the door.

Delilah saw a young woman and man standing outside. She opened the door a crack. "Yes."

"Hi. We're here on behalf of Backer O'Boyle. Can we have a moment of your time?"

"What you want?"

"President O'Boyle is reaching out to citizens in your community. He wants you to know he's working hard for you. He's dedicated himself to making this country fair for everyone, not just the wealthy. People need better jobs, better education, and the president believes if we all work together that change is possible. He asked us to deliver this message to you."

"What you want from me?"

The young woman smiled. "The president doesn't want anything from you. But he does want to know if you're doing all right. In this economy too many people can't buy food or pay their rent."

"Mine gits paid."

The woman looked past Delilah and saw Ronnie sitting on the couch. "Is your boy doing all right? Does he get enough to eat? There are programs available, you know. We have a van on hand to take you down to General Services where someone will help you fill out the paperwork. I can write your name down so the driver picks you up?"

Delilah looked at the young woman for a moment, and then at the young man. "I don't take no welfare."

"You shouldn't look at it like that. It's your money and you have the right to it."

"I have to go to work soon."

"Think it over, and we'll stop by again. If you change your mind, we'll help any way we can. And remember, the president is thinking about you."

CHAPTER THIRTEEN

No one entered or left the Varick Street building as Delsi watched it from across the street. It was pushing six p.m. and she hoped to "accidently" bump into Michael Reny on the street as he was leaving the building. She had not thought through just exactly how to bump into him by accident, but it didn't matter. She had not been able to get him out of her mind and was determined to find out more about him. He was not especially handsome, not in the Hollywood sense; his nose was not perfectly straight, and it looked as though it had been broken and never reset. A couple of his teeth were crooked, but none of it mattered; appearance has nothing to do with a person's character, vision, intellect, or moral attributes. Of course, Delsi was not certain Michael possessed these attributes, but at that moment, she saw only perfection.

The door to the building opened and Michael Reny walked onto the street. It happened suddenly and caught Delsi by surprise. He walked downtown and she followed him for six blocks until he reached the Tribeca Grand Hotel. He stopped at the front desk. Delsi walked past him and stood near the elevator. Reny walked over while reading a message and did not notice her standing there.

"Hello, Michael."

He looked up, startled to see her there, and then smiled. "Are you staying at this hotel?"

"No, I'm not. I waited for you to leave your building and followed you."

He just looked at her. When the elevator door opened, he stepped inside. Delsi followed him. The door closed and they both looked straight ahead. When it opened, Reny stepped out and walked down the hallway. Delsi followed him. He unlocked his door and stepped into the room while Delsi waited in the hallway. Michael gave a small nod and she entered his room.

"Do you usually follow men to their hotel?"

"I don't make a practice of following men at all, if that's what you're asking." Delsi noticed a mahogany bookcase against the far wall and walked over to it. The piece of furniture did not match the décor of the room, and the nicks, chips, and bruises to the wood led her to believe the bookcase belonged to Michael. He must transport it with him in his travels. While the top shelf was reserved for books written in English, the lower shelves all contained books written in foreign languages: French, Portuguese, German and Russian. A few of the authors Delsi noticed included Nietzsche, Marx, and Hawking, to name but a few. One book in particular caught her attention. She removed it from the bookcase and opened it. It was *Steppenwolf* by Hermann Hesse.

"You have a first edition Hermann Hesse? It has to be worth a fortune."

"You enjoy books?"

Delsi closed it and gently slid it back into the bookcase. "Better than most people." She walked over to where Michael was standing. Close enough to look into his eyes much more deeply than she had in their first meeting. His hands hung at his sides. She lifted one and observed it the way a paleontologist would examine a dinosaur bone. His hand was elegant with long spatulated fingers, but it was calloused. "What kind of work did this to you?"

"Swinging a pickaxe in quarries, working in mines and on railroads."

The resonance of his voice struck her. It had a soothing quality to it. She let go of his hand. "Where did you study economics?"

He looked at the books and then back at her. "I never went to college. Traveling, working with your hands, and listening to people is all the teaching one really needs."

Delsi searched his face. "Who are you?"

He smiled and then gave her an inquisitive look. "No one in particular."

She wanted to know everything, but his answers gave her nothing. "Where were you born?"

"Spain, but I'm from Nebraska. My parents were out of the country when I was born."

"And your father? What is his profession?"

"A businessman who traveled. My mother refused to be without him, so she traveled too."

"Are they in Nebraska?"

"No. They're gone."

"I'm sorry. Are you married?"

"No."

An impulse ran through her body to kiss him. Would he object? If not, the urge within her might grow more aggressive. Instead, she stepped back. Her expression tightened, and then softened. She looked directly into his eyes.

He wondered what she was thinking, and in particular, why she had come to his room. His exposure to a wide variety of people had honed his ability to categorize an individual with relative ease, but not Delsi. Her gestures, manner and, for lack of a better word, quirkiness, made her difficult to describe in simple terms.

Delsi's urge to pull him close and kiss him did not wane. She would offer no resistance if he threw her onto the bed and tore her clothes off. As she lay totally naked, he would strip down and fall on top of her, her nails clawing into his arms, his back, his legs. She would swim in his eyes as he made love to her. Standing before him, a lifetime of unrequited passion had exploded inside of her for the first time ever. "I have to leave."

Delsi ran from his room and took the stairs to the lobby. She walked down Varick Street not recalling if she'd said goodbye to him. It mattered little. She had entered a realm that felt both odd and complete, and with someone who was virtually a stranger to her. Till now, she had lived for herself, alone; never had a soul touched her heart in any important way. She retreated to her apartment, an empty cavern, and pondered how it was possible for this man to have filled a void within her she'd never known? No, void was the wrong word, she thought. Her life was complete before meeting Michael, but now, something she never believed she could want had revealed itself. If he wanted her as well, life could take on an entirely new meaning for her.

CHAPTER FOURTEEN

Michael Reny, Charlie and Robert were the first to arrive in the conference room. Delsi showed up shortly afterwards. Excitement charged the air as they waited for Reny to begin his presentation. They all wanted to know why the Fortune 500 CEOs have decided to leave the country.

Reny jotted down one last note on a sheet of paper and then dropped his pen on the table. He looked across at the three seated opposite him. "It has always amazed me how quickly a destructive force can strike, and death blows are usually the ones you never see coming. Let me give you an example. On Christmas day 1991, as the world went to sleep that night, the U.S.S.R. was, to their account, the most powerful country in the world. When we awoke the next morning, they no longer existed. Not one economist, analyst or intelligence bureau had predicted their collapse. It happened quickly and decisively, and their demise devastated the economies of a dozen or so satellite countries that depended on them for financial support and military protection. History is filled with cataclysmic events like this one. And, of course, no country ever believes this fate will thoroughly ravage their empire.

"Now, what actually led to the downfall of the Soviet Union is a subject for another time. In our three meetings we'll be focused strictly on the United States." Reny walked to the window and looked out. "At the heart of all great economic gain or loss is what I call an *event*. This event can catapult a nation to unheralded heights, or devour that same nation in the blink of an eye. An event has three elements. I'll explain each one as they relate to the impending departure of the Fortune 500."

"Excuse me," Robert said. "Can you give an example of an event? I'm not sure I'm following what you're saying."

Reny turned and looked at him. "Elvis Presley."

Robert laughed. "Are you serious?"

"Even Elvis can be explained in socio-economic terms. Three elements in time and space came together to propel Elvis to stardom. The first was music—blues, jazz and gospel music had been around a long time but had never crossed over into the listening tastes and preferences of mainstream America. The second element was an era of rebellion in the '50s. White teenagers, tired of their parent's music and values, were waiting for something—*any*thing—that would allow them to bust loose. Then the third force emerged, the catalyst. He was young, handsome, and had a voice like no singer before him. He loved blues, jazz and gospel, and he had a style all his own. He lit the match, the world caught fire, and no one ever looked back. As you are aware, some elements are around for a long time. Sometimes two of them are. But it takes that unique third element to bring the others together to make an event. At some point, rock and roll would have taken root. But it never would have exploded onto the scene with such force and immediacy if Elvis had not appeared to launch it. And that's what an event creates."

"Do they teach this at Harvard?" Charlie asked.

"I know of no institution that teaches it." Reny looked at his watch. "Let's get started. But before I do, I want to list the topics I will not discuss in our meetings. I have no axe to grind with any political party, so I will not disparage any of them. I try to limit conjecture when supporting my findings. When making a point, if I mention a politician by name, it is not for the purpose of singling him or her out. You'll find that I typically try to balance it out by referring to politicians of the other party. In the same vein I dislike the terms 'he said/she said' or 'good guy/bad guy.'

"A great deal of what you are about to hear, you have heard before. All I'm doing is putting this information in the order in which it should be understood. The problem today is that we are bombarded with so much information that we react to each news bulletin or breaking news story. We, as citizens, have been disarmed and no longer filter the steady flow of information that showers us daily. What I have done is to filter out the non-essential, peel off layers of misdirection, and expose the underlying facts. Only after these elements are brought to the surface will it be possible to grasp the direction this country is moving in.

"It is often said that the most difficult problems have the simplest answers. It is with this belief that I now begin."

Charlie, Robert, and Delsi waited eagerly as Michael Reny paused for a moment to organize his thoughts.

"Element one. Ill-fated decisions by American presidents and Congress have led this country to become debt-ridden."

Reny placed material on the table for them to review. "This chart shows spending during the administrations from Woodrow Wilson to Backer O'Boyle. Look carefully at the cumulative debt created over the last hundred years."

Year	President	Added to / Subtracted from National Debt	Cumulative Debt
1913	Wilson	$47,831,039.50	$2,916,204,913.66
1914	Wilson	-$3,705,644.50	$2,912,499,269.16
1915	Wilson	$145,637,604.00	$3,058,136,873.16
1916	Wilson	$551,107,389.00	$3,609,244,262.16
1917	Wilson	$2,108,526,017.36	$5,717,770,279.52
1918	Wilson	$8,874,391,134.48	$14,592,161,414.00
1919	Wilson	$12,798,808,699.12	$27,390,970,113.12
1920	Wilson	-$1,438,513,706.96	$25,952,456,406.16
1921	Harding	-$1,975,005,853.62	$23,977,450,552.54
1922	Harding	-$1,014,068,844.23	$22,963,381,708.31
1923	Coolidge	-$613,674,342.95	$22,349,707,365.36
1924	Coolidge	-$1,098,894,375.87	$21,250,812,989.49
1925	Coolidge	-$734,619,101.59	$20,516,193,887.90
1926	Coolidge	-$872,977,572.71	$19,643,216,315.19
1927	Coolidge	-$1,131,309,383.34	$18,511,906,931.85
1928	Coolidge	-$907,613,730.42	$17,604,293,201.43
1929	Hoover	-$673,204,717.33	$16,931,088,484.10
1930	Hoover	-$745,778,652.67	$16,185,309,831.43
1931	Hoover	$615,971,660.28	$16,801,281,491.71
1932	Hoover	$2,685,720,952.42	$19,487,002,444.13
1933	Roosevelt	$3,051,670,116.02	$22,538,672,560.15
1934	Roosevelt	$4,514,468,854.33	$27,053,141,414.48
1935	Roosevelt	$1,647,751,210.05	$28,700,892,624.53
1936	Roosevelt	$5,077,650,869.20	$33,778,543,493.73
1937	Roosevelt	$2,646,070,238.56	$36,424,613,732.29

Year	President	Added to / Subtracted from National Debt	Cumulative Debt
1938	Roosevelt	$740,126,583.16	$37,164,740,315.45
1939	Roosevelt	$3,274,792,095.66	$40,439,532,411.11
1940	Roosevelt	$2,527,998,626.57	$42,967,531,037.68
1941	Roosevelt	$5,993,912,498.03	$48,961,443,535.71
1942	Roosevelt	$23,461,001,580.51	$72,422,445,116.22
1943	Roosevelt	$64,273,645,213.68	$136,696,090,329.90
1944	Roosevelt	$64,307,296,891.23	$201,003,387,221.13
1945	Truman	$57,678,800,188.80	$258,682,187,409.93
1946	Truman	$10,739,911,763.33	$269,422,099,173.26
1947	Truman	-$11,135,716,064.59	$258,286,383,108.67
1948	Truman	-$5,994,136,595.68	$252,292,246,512.99
1949	Truman	$478,113,347.34	$252,770,359,860.33
1950	Truman	$4,586,992,490.71	$257,357,352,351.04
1951	Truman	-$2,135,375,536.11	$255,221,976,814.93
1952	Truman	$3,883,201,970.50	$259,105,178,785.43
1953	Eisenhower	$6,965,882,853.14	$266,071,061,638.57
1954	Eisenhower	$5,188,537,469.89	$271,259,599,108.46
1955	Eisenhower	$3,114,623,694.16	$274,374,222,802.62
1956	Eisenhower	-$1,623,409,153.30	$272,750,813,649.32
1957	Eisenhower	-$2,223,641,752.89	$270,527,171,896.43
1958	Eisenhower	$5,816,045,849.38	$276,343,217,745.81
1959	Eisenhower	$8,362,689,332.41	$284,705,907,078.22
1960	Eisenhower	$1,624,853,770.15	$286,330,760,848.37
1961	Kennedy	$2,640,177,761.68	$288,970,938,610.05
1962	Kennedy	$9,229,884,110.82	$298,200,822,720.87
1963	Kennedy	$7,658,810,275.54	$305,859,632,996.41
1964	Johnson	$5,853,266,260.89	$311,712,899,257.30
1965	Johnson	$5,560,999,726.34	$317,273,898,983.64
1966	Johnson	$2,633,188,811.84	$319,907,087,795.48
1967	Johnson	$6,313,849,999.06	$326,220,937,794.54
1968	Johnson	$21,357,468,631.34	$347,578,406,425.88

Year	President	Added to / Subtracted from National Debt	Cumulative Debt
1969	Nixon	$6,141,847,415.53	$353,720,253,841.41
1970	Nixon	$17,198,453,108.52	$370,918,706,949.93
1971	Nixon	$27,211,037,505.61	$398,129,744,455.54
1972	Nixon	$29,130,716,484.96	$427,260,460,940.50
1973	Nixon	$30,881,144,371.59	$458,141,605,312.09
1974	Ford	$16,918,210,419.46	$475,059,815,731.55
1975	Ford	$58,129,184,268.45	$533,189,000,000.00
1976	Ford	$87,244,000,000.00	$620,433,000,000.00
1977	Carter	$78,407,000,000.00	$698,840,000,000.00
1978	Carter	$72,704,000,000.00	$771,544,000,000.00
1979	Carter	$54,975,000,000.00	$826,519,000,000.00
1980	Carter	$81,182,000,000.00	$907,701,000,000.00
1981	Reagan	$90,154,000,000.00	$997,855,000,000.00
1982	Reagan	$144,179,000,000.00	$1,142,034,000,000.00
1983	Reagan	$235,176,000,000.00	$1,377,210,000,000.00
1984	Reagan	$195,056,000,000.00	$1,572,266,000,000.00
1985	Reagan	$250,837,000,000.00	$1,823,103,000,000.00
1986	Reagan	$302,199,616,658.42	$2,125,302,616,658.42
1987	Reagan	$224,974,274,294.58	$2,350,276,890,953.00
1988	Reagan	$252,060,821,088.16	$2,602,337,712,041.16
1989	McBush	$255,093,248,146.16	$2,857,430,960,187.32
1990	McBush	$375,882,491,589.93	$3,233,313,451,777.25
1991	McBush	$431,989,899,919.78	$3,665,303,351,697.03
1992	McBush	$399,317,303,824.63	$4,064,620,655,521.66
1993	McClinton	$346,868,227,617.72	$4,411,488,883,139.38
1994	McClinton	$281,261,026,873.94	$4,692,749,910,013.32
1995	McClinton	$281,232,990,696.07	$4,973,982,900,709.39
1996	McClinton	$250,828,038,426.34	$5,224,810,939,135.73
1997	McClinton	$188,335,072,261.61	$5,413,146,011,397.34
1998	McClinton	$113,046,997,500.28	$5,526,193,008,897.62
1999	McClinton	$130,077,892,717.81	$5,656,270,901,615.43

Year	President	Added to / Subtracted from National Debt	Cumulative Debt
2000	McClinton	$17,907,308,271.43	$5,674,178,209,886.86
2001	McBush	$133,285,202,313.20	$5,807,463,412,200.06
2002	McBush	$420,772,553,397.10	$6,228,235,965,597.16
2003	McBush	$554,995,097,146.46	$6,783,231,062,743.62
2004	McBush	$595,821,633,586.70	$7,379,052,696,330.32
2005	McBush	$553,656,965,393.18	$7,932,709,661,723.50
2006	McBush	$574,264,237,491.73	$8,506,973,899,215.23
2007	McBush	$500,679,473,047.25	$9,007,653,372,262.48
2008	McBush	$1,017,071,524,650.01	$10,024,724,896,912.49
2009	O'Boyle	$1,885,104,106,599.26	$11,909,829,003,511.75
2010	O'Boyle	$1,651,794,027,380.04	$13,561,623,030,891.79
2011	O'Boyle	$1,228,717,297,665.36	$14,790,340,328,557.15
2012	O'Boyle	$954,020,371,507.70	$16,415,769,788,215.80
2017*		$998,020,371,507.70*	$21,622,673,346,690.20*

*Projected U.S. deficit and debt.

"Element one had not surfaced as a volatile element until recently, when debt levels have simply exploded. Here's the mindset of a few of these presidents during their terms in office. Wilson believed himself a man of vision and destiny. So it's no wonder that he was the first president to meddle in the affairs of other nations. Most Americans during Wilson's time were content to stay within the confines of our borders. That was until Wilson launched the nation into World War I. That also launched the practice of running up enormous national debt. The belief on the part of our leaders then—and today, as well—was that the U.S. is a wealthy and powerful country. The thinking is that we can afford to spend and place the nation into debt because we'll pay down the debt at some point.

"President Lyndon Johnson was warned by many advisors, and even the French government, that the Vietnam War was not winnable. But Johnson thought the United States had won two world wars, and to defeat Vietnam would require minimal effort by our military. Besides, to pull our troops out of that country would be an embarrassment to our great nation. So Johnson spent another $40 billion, and he did so at the same time the Civil Rights Act of 1964 was passed. New programs such as the Economic Opportunity Act, Head Start, Medicare, Medicaid, and the Jobs Corps also came into existence at that time, and they all required considerable money and resources. With all this, government had to grow, and some in Washington questioned the soundness of increasing overhead with all this new expense. But the president and his supporters pointed out that the United States was the richest country in the world, and we could afford to pay for our war and also support all those new programs.

"Let's skip to Nixon, the architect of a decision that helped accelerate our ability to accumulate debt. His administration abandoned the gold standard. Up to this point in time, countries that held American dollars could exchange them for our gold. We feared this practice would deplete our gold reserves, which are the largest in the world. The U.S. told the rest of the world that our dollar does not need to be secured by anything except trust in America, and that we would no longer honor the dollar-for-gold swap. There were many reasons Nixon issued this executive order. I won't go into them, but most economists agree that it was the right thing to do for the United States.

"The side effect of Nixon breaking from the gold standard was that future presidents and Congress were now unshackled, and no longer needed to print money based on the value or amount of gold sitting in our coffers. In essence, the government was free to print money anytime they wanted. Looking at our current debt, it's fair to say Washington ran amuck at that point; there were no longer obstructions to paying for our wars or to stop anyone from financing mountains of new programs for the poor. Once again, our presidents and Congress believed that we could afford the mounting debt.

"Presidents are hired to make critical decisions at critical times. Kennedy is the prime example; he told the U.S.S.R to remove their nuclear missile from Cuba or their violation of the Monroe Doctrine would be considered an act of war. The result? They removed their missile. Outside of a few presidents such as Washington, Lincoln, and Kennedy, this country hasn't fared well with presidents confronted with critical decision making. We could run down president by president, but we haven't the time. So let's cover the critical judgment ability of our last three presidents.

"McClinton missed his opportunity to show his critical judgment ability when a call came into the White House from Brooksley Born, the Chairperson of the Commodity Futures Trading Commission. She had called to warn the president that unregulated, over-the-counter derivatives were being traded, and if action was not taken to regulate them, the trading practice could undo the American economy. At the time the economy was booming. Unemployment was low and people from all socio-economic classes were buying homes in record numbers. If McClinton were to regulate sub-prime loans he risked slowing down the economy. This would not benefit McClinton, who wanted his legacy to be his creation of the greatest economy in the history of this country. The fact that our economy was sitting on a bubble waiting to burst played little in his critical judgment. So when Greenspurn and other cronies told him the market would correct itself, it became an easy choice for him to remain quiet and do nothing. No further examination of sub-prime lending was pursued.

"Of course the bubble burst during McBush's term in office and, as we know, he was blamed for the second greatest recession this country has ever seen. He, too, had the opportunity to regulate sub-prime trading, but his focus remained on the two wars he'd started that added another six trillion to our national debt. With certainty, both McClinton and McBush lacked the degree of critical decision making that one expects from a commander-in-chief. I sometimes wonder, perhaps naïvely, if McClinton ever lies awake at night thinking about the trillions of dollars in damage he could have prevented or the hardship he could have averted for millions of Americans had he only placed the country first, and his legacy second. As for McBush's critical judgment, he thought he'd be out of Afghanistan and Iraq in a matter of months, even though, as with Johnson and the Vietnam War, the experts told him it was not possible.

"Aren't you being a little too critical?" Robert said.

"Not if we hold our presidents to the highest standards, as we did with JFK. Not if we expect them to make tough decisions when it matters most. It's what every American expects—and deserves—from their president. And running this country in the black is certainly what the Fortune 500 expected." Reny took a sip of water before looking at his watch. "Is this making sense, or does it sound like dribble?"

"I certainly wouldn't call it dribble," Charlie said. "But I'm still waiting for the big picture."

"I need to wrap up and leave for another meeting. But a few words on President Backer O'Boyle first." Reny clasped his hands together. "He did not start the two wars, but to his credit he's gotten us out of one and reduced our troops and presence in the other. That would be commendable if the story ended there. But it doesn't. When O'Boyle came into office the national debt was $10.5 trillion; with little effort he's driven it over the $16 trillion mark. It appears he has no real desire to slash spending, stating that it would create a hardship on too many people if drastic cuts are made. So how does the debt get paid down? Unfortunately, it's a question lacking a satisfactory answer."

"Do you know the answer?" Robert asked.

"The country paid down its substantial debt after the First and Second World Wars. Our current debt may never be paid down. I see nothing from the president or Congress that will effectively slow down their spending, and this president sees nothing wrong with paying our bills by raising the debt ceiling, printing money at will, or borrowing from foreign nations. I'm jumping ahead here, but I'm doing so because this debt will fall heavily on the Fortune 500. You'll see this point more clearly when we discuss the final two elements. To encapsulate element one: All presidents, along with Congress, have done irreparable damage to this country by running up an ungodly amount of debt."

"Presidents have always run up debt and mismanaged our affairs," Charlie said. "What could ever change that?"

"For one thing, presidential elections should not strictly be a popularity contest. The bar needs to be set much higher, and candidates need to prove they understand finance, business and economics. Primaries are the vehicle to give voters the opportunity to learn all they can about a candidate before they vote them into office. How can that be accomplished when candidates seal their college records and keep important history of their past hidden from the public? Knowing a candidate had never taken a business course or Econ. 101 while in college might sway more than one voter's decision."

"Are you speaking about our current president?" Robert said.

"Let's say this is a topic for another discussion. What's important to know is that most presidential candidates hide their deficiencies from the public, as long as they can get away with it. It's incumbent upon the people to demand complete disclosure on the part of the candidates, with a penalty of disqualification or even impeachment if damaging or erroneous information comes to light by sources other than the candidate. These presidents, and Congress for that matter, cannot continue to drive this country into ruin. The American people must figure out how to demand excellence from anyone entering public office. Anyway, I got off track here by giving you my opinion, but I hope it answers your question."

"I have one more topic to discuss before you leave," Charlie said. "If the Fortune 500 leaves this country, we're going to hell in a hand basket."

"I understand the severity of what's going to happen, Charlie, but corporations are not people. They don't care, they don't love, and they don't hate. They exist to create wealth, for themselves, their stockholders, and employees. At this particular moment in history, they can create wealth more easily in Canada."

"They'll get boycotted if they try to leave," Robert said.

"On the surface it would appear that these companies are committing corporate suicide by moving to Canada, but the majority of them have a strong global presence. And, yes, some will see a drop in profits from the backlash of a boycott. Understand, the research has been done, the models have been charted, and every study conclusively shows that any decline in productivity will be short lived, mostly because people are creatures of habit and want the best value for their dollar, not to mention those who depend on exclusive products, such as medication, that they can only receive from the drug manufacturer that developed it. The expectation is that in six months most people will forget the boycott existed at all and begin purchasing from these companies again."

"How many are expected to leave?" Delsi asked.

While Reny had not avoided looking at Delsi throughout the meeting, he did maintain a strictly professional demeanor toward her. Till now she had remained quiet for most of the meeting. She had left his hotel room rather abruptly the night before. Reny had no way to tell what was going through her mind at that moment, but he thought her low-key disposition as she sat across the table from him was perhaps the result of simple embarrassment from having imposed herself upon him as she had.

"The number of companies is growing, Delsi, and there's a reason for it. If even one hundred of them leave, the negative impact will cause the stock market to tumble. Any company that remains in the U.S. will see their stock value decimated. As a result, each day more and more companies notify us that they have decided to join those relocating to Canada. I would not be surprised if all five hundred decide to move there."

"This is madness!" Charlie said. "Delsi created a model of what will happen if only two hundred and fifty companies leave the U.S. If her model is even half way correct, we're looking at the total collapse of our economy. It might even throw the world into a severe depression."

Reny looked at Delsi, and had a new found respect for her. "I'd be interested in seeing your model, Delsi. As for the collapse spreading across the world, Charlie, I wouldn't overly worry. Yes, the global markets will suffer the blow, but since the 500 will no longer be traded on any of the U.S. exchanges, their stock value will avoid being decimated. They will be impacted to a larger degree, and within sixty to ninety days they will stabilize, as will the other markets around the world. The U.S. unfortunately will suffer the most damage." Reny looked at his watch. "I'm already late, and I need to leave this very moment."

"When will you present element two?"

"It has to happen soon," Reny said. "I'm getting pressure from the 500 committee to get things going. Let's meet tomorrow at 7:30 a.m."

Charlie looked around the table and there was no push back. "Tomorrow morning it is."

Reny bundled up his material and stashed it into his briefcase. He headed to the door. Before leaving he stopped and turned to Charlie. "Have you looked up Ralph Bunche?"

CHAPTER FIFTEEN

Delsi flagged a taxi on Varick Street outside the building. Charlie headed uptown with her.

"I know of Ralph Bunche," Charlie said. "But what does Reny expect me to uncover about the man?"

Delsi knew just about everything there was to know about Ralph Bunche, including where she suspected Michael Reny was leading Charlie. But it was not her place to mention the critical four words that came to mind when the name Ralph Bunche was mentioned. She was certain those words still carried the same relevance they did seventy years ago. Eleanor Roosevelt had often expressed them, but when Ralph Bunche spoke them they resonated in a way that few others could equal.

"Reny's got me curious. I'll have to do some research when I get the time," Charlie said. He looked at his watch. "Angela's show opens tonight and I'm meeting her family for dinner first."

"Thanks for keeping me in the loop, and for those center aisle tickets, too."

"I apologize. I should have thought about Robert and you. I've been a little distracted lately."

Delsi was aware he had not been himself since losing his seat in the Senate, and she suspected his separation from Angela had taken its toll on him as well. Maybe taking on a pressure-packed project was not the right thing now. "You must be proud of Angela, now that she's on the stage again."

"I'm very proud." Charlie motioned for the driver to pull over at Seventh Avenue and Forty-sixth Street. "Sorry we can't chat longer. I need to run. I'll see you bright and early." He stepped out in front of the Lunt-Fontanne Theatre on West Forty-sixth. Marcus and Charisa were standing there with most of the Robinson family. Marcus had picked up Kaitlin as promised. When she saw her daddy, she flew into his arms.

"You're getting so big I can hardly lift you."

Kaitlin was not about to be set down. She laid her head on his shoulder to get a much needed hug.

"Let's head over to the restaurant," Marcus said.

They entered Trattoria Trecolori on West Forty-seventh Street. A long table had been set up to seat twenty-two members of the Robinson family. Charlie ordered his favorite: *fritto misto*, a fried medley of calamari and shrimp garnished with fried zucchini and peppers served with a *fra diavolo* sauce. Kaitlin got a half order of spaghetti and two meatballs, and Charlie showed her the art of winding spaghetti onto her fork.

When they were done eating, the family remained at the table a while longer to enjoy each other's company. The chit-chat went on for a while, until Marcus noticed the clock on the wall.

"We got to go! Angela's show starts in ten minutes."

* * *

Critics such as Charles Isherwood and Ben Brantley had attended the previews of *Once Upon A Time* and gave the show great reviews. Both reviews mentioned Angela as a force to be reckoned with in the show. It opened with the number "Straighten Up and Fly Right" made popular in 1944 by Nat King Cole. It was followed by the Ink Spots hit "I'll Get By (As Long As I Have You)," and then five more greats from the '40s. The next set kicked off the '50s with the Platters hits "Only You (And You Alone)," and "The Great Pretender." Next came "Jailhouse Rock" by Elvis Presley and "You Send Me" by Sam Cook. A number of other hits from the '50s were also sung.

When it came time for the '60s music, Kaitlin grabbed Charlie's hand and squeezed. Angela appeared at center stage with two back-up singers. She covered the Supremes hit "You Keep Me Hangin' On." Next they sang "Dancing in the Street" by Martha and The Vandellas. Angela's third song, Aretha Franklin's "(You Make Me Feel Like) A Natural Woman" showcased the incredible range in her voice. The audience rose to their feet in applause when she finished that song.

After the show, the whole family waited for Angela at the side door of the theatre. When she walked out Kaitlin ran into her mother's waiting arms.

"You were incredible," Charlie said, and kissed her on the cheek. He stepped aside to allow the rest of the family to congratulate her. Kaitlin had school in the morning and it was already eleven p.m., far past her bedtime. The family dispersed to all points leading to Brooklyn. Charlie, Angela and Kaitlin walked down West Forty-sixth Street. Sleepiness crept into Kaitlin's eyes and Charlie picked her up. Angela flagged a taxi on the corner and slid into the back seat. Charlie handed Kaitlin to Angela and leaned over and kissed her on the lips.

Angela looked into Charlie's eyes and he had to say what was in his heart. "I miss you. Are you coming home soon?"

CHAPTER SIXTEEN

A smile came to Delilah's face when she walked through the front door and saw Ronnie at the coffee table doing his homework. She slipped off her sweater and sat down beside him.

"How was school today?"

"Okay, I guess."

Delilah turned his face toward hers. "What's wrong? You not feelin' well?"

Ronnie turned back to his homework. "It's nothin'."

"Got to be somethin' Why you mopin'?"

"The new sneakers don't fit right."

"What? They you size." Delilah reached under the table and took hold of his foot. She felt the sides of the sneaker and where his big toe was located. "These sneakers fit." Ronnie kept his head down and didn't say anything.

"Someone say somethin' bout your sneakers?"

"Some kids said light blue's a girl's color."

"Blue's a boy's color. Everyone know that."

"Freddie's mom got him Jordan's with red, silver and black on 'em."

"Hmm, and her not workin'." A knock on the door ended the discussion. Delilah told Ronnie to stay on the couch.

When she opened the door, she saw the young woman and man from the week before standing on the porch.

"Hi. We were in the neighborhood and thought we'd say hello," said the woman with a smile. "Our van will be driving people down to vote in a couple of days, and if you need a ride the driver will come to pick you up."

Delilah saw the Backer O'Boyle badge pinned to the young woman's coat. "I don't need no help gettin' to the votin' booth, and so you know, my vote gonna be for Matt Roman. Don't be comin' here no more."

The young woman seemed startled. "Matt Roman represents big business and the wealthy. He'll eliminate entitlements for the poor if he's elected. And he doesn't even believe women have the right to control their own bodies."

"I hear all that, and it sad a young college girl like you taken with it. You go along now, an' I hope you git some sense one day and not believe everythin' people tell ya." Delilah closed the door and walked back to the couch. Ronnie was still moping about the sneakers he had to wear.

"Time you learned what's important." Delilah placed the stool next to the kitchen cabinet and climbed onto it. She opened the cabinet door and pulled down a large crock pot and carried it into the outer room. She removed the lid and Ronnie saw it filled with five- and ten-dollar bills. "This be your college money. No week go by I don't save somethin' for you. *This* important, not no high-priced rubber on you feet."

"I know, Mom, but just once I'd like to have Jordan's."

A flash of anger came into her eyes. "Just because Freddie's mama take that check every month and buy him what he want, don't mean we do. Ain't our way!"

"Why not, Mom?"

She grabbed him by the shoulders. "Your great great granddaddy were a slave. Pickin' cotton for free ain't no different than gittin' a government check. We free, Ronnie. Takin' that check kill my dream for you. It teach you the wrong thing." Delilah sat there a moment to cool herself down. "If others need it, that their business." She put her hand into the crock pot and grabbed a handful of money. All the long hours she'd worked for those dollars allowed her to smile on the inside. She placed the lid on the crock pot and returned it to the top shelf in the cabinet. She returned to the outer room. "Now, what'd you learn in school today?"

CHAPTER SEVENTEEN

Michael Reny arrived at 6:30 a.m. only to be greeted by Delsi when he entered the conference room.

"You're an early bird."

"I brought my model, the one you asked to see." She waited for him to sit across from her. "I based it on two-hundred and fifty corporations leaving the U.S., and calculated how their departure would affect the economy." Delsi turned her laptop to show him her predictions. "This curve reflects the downward spiral as more companies move to Canada."

Reny glanced briefly at her model. "It's correct as far as you've gone, but it's not the whole picture."

"What have I missed?"

"When I have time, I'll add a couple of components for you."

"Add them now."

"I'm hesitant."

"I think that's quite arrogant of you to say so. I've covered everything, so maybe it's you who hasn't looked at it correctly. Let me explain it in more detail."

"No need," Reny said. "I understand your model perfectly."

Delsi stared at him. "Then you see the destruction that will occur, but you don't really care what happens to this country. That's what you're telling me?"

"Caring is within my ability, but changing history is not."

"You talk like this is a fait accompli. That nothing can change what's going to happen to this country. I find that hard to believe."

Reny sat back. "May I tell you a story?"

Delsi felt he was patronizing her. If there was one thing she found distasteful, it was a know-it-all who believed they had the answers for everything. "I'd be interested to hear your story."

"In 1984 my father took me to Wang Laboratories, headquartered in Lowell, Massachusetts. I was in grammar school at the time, and it was a trip I'll never forget. Here was this large computer company that dominated word processing automation and had thirty-three thousand employees with offices all over the world. I remember meeting Dr. An Wang, a warm and personable man, and an innovator whose brilliance had built the company from the ground up. My father had gone to Lowell at his request. As they stood there speaking, I remember my father asking Dr. Wang why he hadn't embraced PC technology earlier. The business world was converting to this new platform at the speed of light because it offered a cost-effective solution, and for employees it was much easier to operate. Dr. Wang told him that PC technology did not possess the horsepower that companies needed to operate their businesses, and it would be only a matter of time before those companies discarded PC technology and returned to mini computers.

"When we left the building that day and walked to our car, my father told me to turn around and look at the Wang towers. After I did, he said, "They don't know it yet, but this company is already out of business." We got into our car and drove away. Every now and then I think back to standing in the hallways of the Wang building, with people rushing past me in this bustling, thriving environment, but, as my father pointed out, the company was already out of business, a ghost lingering until the day it was told it no longer had life. As the business died a slow, horrible death, Wang scurried to bring in highly touted executives who promised to turn things around, but nothing ever came of it. Customers left like rats abandoning a sinking ship. Finally, in 1997, Wang went under."

Michael placed his hands on the table and leaned toward Delsi. "It's hard for any human to rationalize that something so horrible could happen to the country they love. More so, to know in advance that she will disappear before your very eyes. My father took me to Wang that day so I would see firsthand the loss of a large and powerful corporation, and to teach me an important lesson: the seeds of destruction are visible to us all, if we only open our eyes to them. But left alone to grow, these seeds will one day crumble even the most powerful dynasty."

Delsi had nothing to say. She was no longer angry with him. They sat in silence until Charlie and Robert walked into the room.

"Morning, Delsi," Charlie said. "What are you looking at there?"

"I brought my model for Michael to look over."

Charlie was about to set his Starbucks down, but he paused to ask Reny, "What do you think of her work?"

"It's quite good," Reny said.

"And her conclusions?"

Reny looked at Delsi, and then back at Charlie. "She's got it right."

A look of despair came to Charlie's face as he set his coffee down and took a seat. "I'll need to call the president."

"I agree," Robert said. "Someone's got to fix this, and fast."

Reny looked at them. "You're going through denial. It's only natural. No rational person would believe a cataclysmic event is about to destroy this country. But, before you run off, I suggest you hear the other two elements. They may give you a different perspective. And, of course, I want to remind you that I'm holding these meetings because I still want you to negotiate the land purchase with Canada."

"Actually," Charlie said. "I need some clarity on that. Why don't you negotiate the deal?"

"I'm not a negotiator. I want someone with integrity to handle what might become one of the most important real estate transactions in history. Secondly, a large team needs to handle the migration of corporations and their people into Canada. I want you to lead that effort as well, Charlie. This is why I'm taking this time to explain the event to you. One other thing—and I don't say this to be cruel—but nothing can reverse the event. It would be futile to exhaust your energy trying to come up with a workaround that will keep these companies from leaving the U.S. Do you recall my opening remark to you? The U.S.S.R. disappeared overnight." Reny now looked at Delsi. "In my model, the United States will not totally disappear, but she will suffer a severe wound and require much care if she is ever to survive."

He paused a moment. "Now, rumors have already spread that a large group of companies are planning to leave the country. The press media is buzzing, but they don't have any solid information to put out yet. Once they do, all hell will break loose. So, listen closely, because we don't have much time.

"To recap, element one documented the government's penchant for spending inordinate amounts of money on wars, domestic programs, foreign aid, and to support the largest number of government employees ever assembled. As spending increases and money dissipates, our government continues to raise the debt ceiling, borrow trillions more, and print money with the belief our country can absorb the added debt, and a deeper belief that someday we will figure out how to pay off this debt. A point I did not make earlier is that our elected officials believe it is the responsibility of the United States to lift mankind out of poverty, to police the world, and to become the model for every other country to emulate. All noble deeds, but no one nation has the resources to maintain the spending level required for such high-minded goals. I should add that the only possible outcome for any country that travels down this course is bankruptcy. The interest alone that the U.S. will pay on its mounting debt is just shy of $1 trillion a year, and within thirty-six months this interest payment will become our largest, single, yearly expenditure. I cannot underscore the magnitude this burden places on the United States.

"Let's move to the second element now." Reny paused to allow his guests time to digest what he had just told them. He also wanted to see the eager look in their eyes before starting up again. "Rarely does a day go by when one political party fails to demagogue the other, and any hope that these parties will find the middle ground to negotiate even the most inane issue has all but gone. These United States have become more polarized today than at any other time in history. What we fail to realize is that the early stage of a civil war is upon us, but one quite different from the war of Lincoln. This new war has elements that have existed for ages: a society where the less fortunate consider themselves marginalized by the wealthy. Like most grievances, the truth does exist to a greater or lesser degree, depending on whose side you are on. Government has taken the side of the poor and become their protector. Capitalists believe a robust economy can raise the poor and solidify the middle class.

"There is the growing divide with roots deep and strong, and it is aided by every news anchor, politician, pundit, and person on the street who argues one side or the other each day. We allow ourselves to believe things will improve because that is the direction we expect such matters to take. But, day-to-day living and working is demanding on most people and precludes them from filtering in any effective way the slanted news forced upon them each and every night. Gone are the days of Edward R. Murrow and Walter Cronkite. A time past when Americans trusted those who delivered news to them. The truth is we no longer place much trust in our news anchors. Each one peels back the layer of news they want us to see, or not to see. So, in part because of them, because of their agenda, their political leaning, or that of their network, the truth stays partially hidden, and it's a sin, because the one truth all anchors need to report is that we are at the beginning of a civil war. Clearly, it is a war that has been officially declared.

"Now, a civil war by its very nature has a line drawn in the dirt with both sides refusing to budge an inch. In this case, the liberal left, the conservative right, and all groups in between have entrenched themselves on one side of the issue or the other. Even the president has clearly declared his side. The issue at stake is as old as the hills and has never died. The poor and the middle class believe they own this country. In his Gettysburg Address Abraham Lincoln made it clear that we have a 'government of the people, by the people, for the people.' He said ours is a government by the *consent* of the people, and a government agreed to through a written contract called a constitution.

"Big business believes this country is founded upon the principles of free enterprise, laissez-faire, and the belief that each man has been given the liberty to pursue his own happiness. No man with a vision or dream shall be ripped asunder by those who rage against him out of their own envy, pettiness, or lack of ability. God has given them an inalienable right to seek their destiny. Let them now go and find it.

"Below these two lofty ideals are the spoils. And they will go to the victor." Reny paused and looked at the three people sitting in front of him. "The time has come when a decisive victor will grab power and go unchallenged, possibly for generations."

"Are you saying one political party will dominate the other?"

"Right now the country is split down the middle, but here's what makes this second element relevant and note-worthy. There are three main demographics among voting groups. Two are minority and the other is the group with the majority of voters. U.S. citizens for one minority group numbered 22.5 million in 1990. That number grew to 52 million by 2011, and by 2050 there will be 132 million of this minority group living in the United States. The other minority group has 42 million citizens right now; by 2050 their number will grow to 66 million. The majority group currently has 220 million citizens. Over the next fifty years, however, their birth rates are projected to drop by fifty percent below their current birth rate. But it won't take fifty years for demographics to change the power structure of voting in this country. Combine the minority, blue collar, union, liberal, and college-age student votes, and you have fifty-three percent of the popular vote. If a presidential candidate wins the popular vote, he usually wins the election. This explains why, in the last election, minority groups played a major role in deciding who would occupy the White House.

"Moderate conservatives believe their party can survive if they court one of the minority voting groups, thinking that will level the playing field in upcoming elections. What they fail to understand is that time has run out on them. Had they planned this strategy a decade ago it might have allowed them to maintain political relevance. The fact of the matter is that voting power in our country has changed forever. It will never resemble any previous period of our past, and even though the two-party system will remain intact, one party has emerged as the dominant force with the power to elect whomever they want, whenever they want. That includes the power to make new laws and repeal laws not deemed in their best interest. The question now becomes: what kind of America will they choose for us?"

Reny's cell phone rang. "Yes." He listened a moment then walked into the hallway to continue his conversation in private. He returned five minutes later. "Something has come up. I have to leave. I'll complete the second element and cover the third in our next and final meeting." He looked at Charlie. "You need to think hard about everything. There's little time to spare, so once I've completed the third element, I'll need an answer from you within twenty-four hours. Either you come aboard, or you don't. Are we clear?"

* * *

Even before Reny had time to pack up his things, Charlie was up and out the door.

"Where's he off to in such a hurry?" Robert said, as he accompanied Delsi into the hallway.

"I'm not sure. He didn't say anything to me. I thought he'd want to recap what we heard today." As Delsi spoke, she kept one eye on the conference room door. She wanted to see when Michael Reny left the room.

"Want to grab something to eat?"

"I'm not hungry, Robert."

"We can go over what Reny discussed today."

"I'm not comfortable talking in a restaurant. Walls have ears."

"We can go somewhere quiet, out of the way."

Delsi gave him a queer look. "And where might that be?"

"Anywhere we can talk in private. My place, your place?"

Reny walked out of the conference room and headed out of the building. "I've got to go, Robert, maybe another time."

Delsi left the building just moments after Reny. He walked south on the avenue and appeared to be headed back to his hotel. She stayed a respectable distance behind him. If he happened to turn and see her, he might think she was stalking him. His abrupt ending of their meeting had intrigued her. She suspected something important was about to take place. Reny reached his hotel. Outside, he was greeted by two men. After shaking hands and chatting for a moment, Reny escorted them inside and into the elevator. Delsi approached the elevator bank. She asked herself whether she should continue spying on him or not. When the elevator door opened, however, she stepped inside and pressed the button for his floor, assuming they went to Michael Reny's room.

There was no one in the hallway when Delsi got off the elevator. She proceeded to Reny's door and heard muffled voices in the room. She looked up and down the hallway once more to make sure she was alone, and then pressed her ear against his door. The voices were loud and clear, but no one was speaking English, not even Reny. Recalling her one year of Russian studies while at M.I.T., she was both pleased and surprised when she comprehended two words: *economy* and *debt*. She listened intently, but the men were speaking too quickly. She realized she had little to gain from standing in the hallway with one ear pressed against Reny's door, so she walked to the elevator, went down and left the hotel. As she walked, she tried to think through this new mystery that had developed. Was Michael Reny a Russian agent? If so, what could he possibly be after? And what on God's earth had compelled her to follow him back to his hotel for a second time? A half block later she remembered her emotions from the night before. Feeling helpless and rendered powerless to control her emotions, she tried to push him out of her mind.

* * *

Charlie went straight from the meeting to Angela's new digs in Tribeca. Her invitation to him was a step in the right direction. The door opened, Angela smiled, and Charlie wasted little time pulling her into his arms. He kissed her, and she kissed him right back.

Once inside he looked around. "Very nice."

"Look, southern exposure. I have my coffee at this table every morning." She walked him down the hallway. "Here's Kaitlin's room."

"She must like all the windows."

Angela pulled him further down the hallway. "And this is mine."

"Wow. Big bedroom." Charlie looked at her with desire in his eyes. He picked her up and carried her to the bed. They lay wrapped in each other's arms for several minutes. It felt good to hold her, but there were no guarantees that she would ever come home.

"Rehearsal is in an hour."

"I know." He kissed her.

Angela gently pulled away. "I'm not ready yet, Charlie."

"When will you be?"

She sat up. "I don't know. It's been a long time since I've felt good about myself, and I feel pretty good right now." She turned to him. "I love you, Charlie, but if we're going to have a life together, I need to know your family comes first, above all else. I could never go through another election campaign, and I would die having to give up my music again. Life is fleeting and I want to enjoy each day of it. This is not an ultimatum, but I need my husband home at night, not out campaigning to save the world."

"I want that, too. More than you know."

She placed her hands on his face. "I do love you, Charlie, but let's take it slow for right now."

"I need to ask you something. Would you ever consider moving away?"

"Moving? To where?"

"To Canada, for instance."

Angela pushed away. "I could never leave my family, Charlie."

CHAPTER EIGHTEEN

Delilah got home from her supermarket job and expected to see Ronnie sitting at the coffee table doing his homework. She was surprised when she saw he wasn't there. She walked into the kitchen where mama was cooking dinner.

"Where's Ronnie?"

"Oh, playin' with the boy next door. Told 'em I'd yell when dinner was ready."

"Mama, I told you never let 'em outside. Not with the gangs and drugs."

The door opened and Ronnie ran into the house with his friend Freddie. "Mom, you on Twitter?"

"Twitter?"

"Look at Freddie's phone. Samuel L. Axon called you somethin'."

"Make sense, boy. What you talkin' about?"

Freddie walked over. "Some woman tweeted that you votin' for Matt Roman, and Samuel L. called you a...well, I better not say."

Delilah placed her hands on her hips. "Go on boy, say it."

Freddie looked at Ronnie, and then back at Delilah. "Samuel L. said you a 'craaazy beeeech.'"

Delilah's jaw dropped. She grabbed his cell phone to look at the messages flashing across the screen. "What in the world?"

"Everyone's talkin' on Twitter, Mom. Once Samuel L. tweeted, the whole country's tweetin' back 'bout you votin' for Roman."

Delilah tried to imagine how that could be. She never talked politics with anyone, and she never told a soul she thought Matt Roman was the best man to turn this country around. Then she remembered the other night when the campaigners came to her door. To get rid of them, she had told the young woman that Roman was getting her vote. "I don't know nothin' bout twittin' or whatever you call it. Ronnie, did you do your homework tonight?"

"Some of it, Mom."

"Well, you git goin' then. And Freddie, you gotta go."

"Yes, Ms. Jones. Should I keep you posted on what twitter's sayin'?"

"I don't give a hill 'a beans 'bout Samuel L. Axon or the rest of 'em. My votin' is my business. You go on now."

"Okay. See you at school, Ronnie."

Delilah waited for Ronnie to leave. "I'm goin' down to vote. Mama, lock the door when I leave, and Ronnie, have you homework done when I git back."

It was a fifteen-minute walk to the school building where Delilah had to vote. She entered and waited in line in the gymnasium. She heard people laughing at the back of the line. When she turned, she saw they were looking at her. Within minutes half the people in line were looking at her and whispering under their breath. When it was Delilah's turn to vote, she showed the woman her identification card and entered the voting booth where she cast her ballot. As she left the gymnasium all eyes were upon her. Delilah held her head high and left the school.

Fifteen minutes later Delilah was back home. Ronnie looked up at her. "It's done, Mom."

Delilah picked up his paper and began to read it over. "What this about?"

"The teacher told us to write two paragraphs about our parents. Where they work and what we do for fun as a family. That kinda stuff."

Delilah was still flustered about all the Twitter nonsense and all the stares and hushed gossiping at the voting booth. As she read Ronnie's paper, however, a smile came to her face. He had written: "My mom works two jobs, one during the day, and one at night. She makes breakfast for me every morning and stays with me outside until the school bus comes. My mom gets home from her first job at seven p.m. and asks what I learned in school each day. After we talk I finish my homework and it's time for bed. My mom reads a story to me. I know all three of them by heart, but when she reads I feel good inside. After she's done she rubs my back and I fall asleep. In the morning my mom wakes me up and then goes to the kitchen and makes my breakfast again. I love my mom because she takes real good care of me."

CHAPTER NINETEEN

Michael Reny did not hear Delsi enter the conference room until she placed her laptop on the table.

"Morning."

Reny looked up. "Morning, Delsi." He continued working on his computer.

"I added a couple more variables to my model last night. Would you like to see it?"

Reny kept his head down and typed. Delsi sat down and waited. A minute or two passed with no response from him.

"When I ratchet up the number of companies to leave the country, some interesting things start to happen." She slid a copy of her analysis across the table.

Reny glanced over at her and then picked up her analysis. He took a quick look at it and slid it back to her. "You continue to impress me, Delsi. What made you think of that?"

"If four hundred companies leave, the U.S. would have no choice but to make drastic cuts. That means pulling our troops out of Japan, Korea and Europe. That would mean, of course, that China would no longer be restrained in the Far East, and Russia would begin making overtures to the European countries. And just like that, the U.S. would no longer be considered a world power by either its allies or its foes. The only foreign country we would continue to support would be Israeli. If we were to withdraw that support, Islam, led by Iran, would issue a *fatwâ* to butcher every man, woman and child in Israel."

Reny pointed at something on her analysis. "How did you figure out this piece?"

"Once the economy crashes and the U.S. is no longer able to pay the interest on the treasury notes held by China and Russia, these countries will demand payment in full. That's a cool three trillion. Of course these two superpowers will want to get paid in gold, because the dollar will be practically worthless. We have to assume the U.S. will never part with its gold. That's when China will make her move to buy Alaska. A fresh influx of capital would give the U.S. some breathing room, but, of course, Russia would also want access to North America. At that point, a bidding war would likely ensue." Delsi stopped there.

"And?" Reny asked.

"On the home front, the nation will already have been brought to its knees. The cost of food will have skyrocketed, jobs will be scarce, and crime will have struck fear into the heart of every American. The U.S. will have no choice but to let Alaska go."

Reny sat back and stared at her across the table. "Many economists waste their time on Keynesian economics while others praise the virtues of Adam Smith. None of them sees a global power shift taking place. None, that is, except you."

"I never would have thought this through if we hadn't met. The question is: How much will the model change after you present the third element?"

Reny was not sure how to answer her. Thoughtfully he said, "It will change even more. But keep this to yourself for the time being, if you don't mind. I want to complete the third element before Charlie and Robert hear anything else."

Delsi nodded. "I need to ask a question."

"I'll answer it if I can."

"Why have you taken the side of big business? You've always fought for the underdog, average men like miners, laborers, and always the less fortunate."

"I'm still fighting for them now, although it might not seem so. This country is about to destroy the corporate world as we know it, and few understand the devastation that will occur. If you've ever studied Karl Marx and his Communist Manifesto, you know his doctrine describes how an agrarian society evolves into a capitalist one until, at some point in history, there's a violent overthrow of capitalism, and socialism and communism reign. Well, it's a great theory and maybe future mankind will embrace a society similar to the one found in Marx's theory, but this world, and especially the U.S., is not prepared to embrace such a society today or even in ten years from now. All things must evolve at their own pace. To force an event before its time leads to sheer destruction. Let me explain.

"When the Bolsheviks took power in 1917, the Communist Manifesto was their driving force. Once Tsar Nicholas II was ousted, the theory of property changed. The people believed that land should be owned by the peasants, by those who worked on the estates, not by the idle rich. And so, a new kind of equality came to pass. Those in power in Russia decided to skip over the capitalist period; in their opinion, Russia had no use for that type of society. Instead, they established a government that went directly into communism. To not allow Russian society to evolve naturally was a huge blunder. Few political decisions in the annals of history can compare with Russia's staggering mistake. I do believe, however, that the U.S. is about to blunder on a similar magnitude. An attempt to destroy capitalism is in the making. Even if Marx was right about the violent but eventual overthrow of capitalism, I don't believe we've reached that point in history just yet.

"I hope you now understand why I approached the Fortune 500 and brought to light that their survival was in jeopardy. To kill corporate profits is tantamount to killing off Third World nations and devastating to hundreds of millions of people around the world.

"You will understand more clearly once I complete the third element." Reny took a sip of water. Delsi, on the other hand, twisted the cap off her bottle and drank most of the contents down. Her eyes remained fixed on Michael as she did so.

"I will share with you one more thing. It has come to Russia's attention that the Fortune 500 companies plan to leave the U.S. They have placed an enticing proposal on the table that has proven quite appealing to the committee. If the committee accepts their proposal, it would be a windfall for Russia. They skipped over capitalism a hundred years ago, and now, to have the Fortune 500 fall into their lap at this time in history, well, it would vindicate one of Russia's greatest blunders. Not to mention, stealing the U.S. economy right out from under America's nose garners the Russians tremendous pleasure."

"American companies would never accept Russia's offer. I don't care what they've put on the table."

"Delsi, keep confidential what I've just shared with you. It's rare when I speak about things that should remain private. Do I have your word?"

"Yes. I do have one more question, though. If you don't want to answer it, just say so. Why Charlie? I know you said he's an honorable man, but there have to be a hundred honorable people you could've picked. Why him?"

Reny leaned back and folded his hands on his lap. "We all need heroes in our lives, people to look up to. For me, Charlie is that hero."

Delsi did not expect that answer. Nor did she expect to hear Michael speak so humbly.

"I know quite a bit about Charlie. Maybe even more than you do," he said. "Most people know him as a United States Senator, but there's much more to him than that. Look at the conditions under which he was brought into this world. He had a less than joyous childhood, one that easily could have led him into despair in later years, but he managed to navigate every roadblock placed before him and survive. At the age of two, Charlie was removed from his home and placed in foster care. The next four years were spent moving from one foster home to another. At age six he was adopted by the Connollys who raised him as their own natural child. It was a real home in a part of town he had never seen before. He finally had parents who loved and taught him to stand tall in this world. He adjusted well. He turned out to be a natural athlete and track star. Rutgers gave him a scholastic scholarship. He excelled both in the classroom and on the field. Then tragedy struck. A car accident took both his parents and Charlie was once again alone in the world. Years later Angela entered his life and became his much needed rock. When Kaitlin came along it made them a family. The rest of the Robinson family was always close by to surround them all with love.

"As a young man, Charlie decided to locate his natural mother. He went from agency to agency until he uncovered her name. Here's one reason why I admire him so much: Most people want to locate their biological parent to learn the truth of why they had been thrown away, or, in Charlie's case, taken away. It's only natural to want to know why this person was unfit as a parent. Not so with Charlie. His only purpose for finding this woman, his mother, was to know if she was suffering. Did she have enough food and clothing? Did she have shelter? Never would Charlie go down the dark path and ask her the usual questions of what happened, why she wasn't a better mother, and why she never came looking for him when social services took him from her. Charlie would never ask those questions because he already knew the answers, and in his heart he had forgiven her. He never did find his mother, and it wasn't for lack of trying. She had simply disappeared in a borough with burnt out buildings and vacant lots. It's where so many poor souls like her were discarded, or where they discarded themselves, and were never to be heard from again.

"I knew some of this," Delsi said. "There were times when I wanted to ask him about his challenges, but it never felt right, so I never asked him."

"I'll answer your initial question now of why I chose Charlie. There are men who belong to a higher order in this world. They cannot be bought or sold or swayed with pieces of gold. They live in a place that most men only dream about, where vision is clear and thought and beliefs are pristine. They know what is true in this world, and they cannot pass injustice by no matter how small. Charlie can no more escape these qualities than he can escape his mortality. So these three meetings come down to this: either Charlie will decide to help transition these corporations and millions of Americans to another country, or he will stay behind to help the less fortunate, using his vision to create a better world. Whichever choice he makes will be the right choice because the world will benefit either way."

"So you're preparing Charlie?"

Michael did not answer her. A moment later Charlie and Robert walked into the room. "Good morning."

"Morning," Delsi said.

Reny shut down his computer and waited until everyone was seated. "Let's see. Earlier I was talking about the U.S. being in the early stages of civil war and the country being divided down the middle. On one side the government believes it must take action to improve the condition of the middle class and poor. This is done primarily by implementing safety net programs for them, and also by regulating the destructive and corrosive tendencies of big business. The other side represents big business. They believe this country was founded on the principles of liberty, free enterprise, and the right to exist without imperious government restrictions. I also covered our evolving demographics and how one political party will dominate voting, and that this new dynamic will determine who lives in the White House for the foreseeable future.

"What you described is not a civil war," Robert said.

"Really? What would you call it?"

"Nothing more than what's been going on since 1776."

"What I described might not seem so severe because we're conditioned to expect one earth-shattering event to occur. And when it does, reality will finally set in. That approach gets you nowhere. But if you allow yourself to filter out those thoughts, you will then see Main Street versus Wall Street: the rapidly growing poor, government versus big business, students versus government and big business, $1 trillion in student loans to be defaulted upon because there are no jobs for graduates, students revolting against universities for exorbitant tuition fees, the 'Occupy Wall Street' movement growing in number each day and spreading to more cities across the country, the 'Occupy Homes' movement physically blocking the take back of underwater houses. I have a dozen more examples of why this period in our history is being called America's autumn. Need I continue?"

"No need. I see your point. But what you also described is people fighting the injustice that's taken over in this country. Without a decent job you can't put food on the table. To make matters worse, big companies are limiting employees to a thirty-hour work week just so they don't have to pay them benefits. Big retailers pay their employees nine dollars an hour, while the heirs of these companies are billionaires. Workers at Wendy's, McDonald's and Burger King are beginning to strike for better pay. Big business is choking the people of this country, and if it weren't for food stamps, I don't know how these people would eat."

Charlie looked at Delsi. "I'm sure you must have something to say."

"Why hasn't O'Boyle corrected these problems? When the sub-prime bubble burst in 2008 and pitted Main Street against Wall Street, not one Wall Street executive was prosecuted. And, yes, big business has been taking advantage of their employees. But how does the president respond to this injustice? By creating crippling regulations to further burden small businesses from paying workers higher wages in addition to handcuffing employers from hiring more workers. Who can afford a hundred thousand dollars in regulation fees to open a pizza shop? Something is terribly wrong when the government lets the crooks walk away and instead punishes the little guy from going into business."

"The perfect segue into element three."

"Element three. In an event, one element has to be the catalyst. In this case it's Backer O'Boyle. Let's look at him more closely. As a child he saw the poor suffer, and he promised himself to one day liberate these people from poverty. His dream was to see the poor move from apartments in crime-infested neighborhoods to homes in safe neighborhoods where their children can attend schools with good teachers. When they're sick they can walk into a hospital and receive the best health care without being turned away,

119

and when they are never denied food or necessities simply because they are poor.

"O'Boyle became a community organizer for Project Vote right after college. He mobilized volunteers to knock on doors in some of the poorest neighborhoods of Chicago. With his glowing charisma he inspired these volunteers to register a whole new demographic of voters. By 1992 these voters numbered in the tens of thousands. They helped to elect McClinton president. O'Boyle had a glimpse of power for the first time when the poor followed him. He experienced power again when the middle class and wealthy did the same. He went on to graduate from law school and become a civil rights attorney.

"O'Boyle enjoyed no greater pleasure than to help the poor in a world which he viewed as decidedly unfair to the underprivileged. Later he became a professor and taught constitutional law, but he never forgot the impact of his triumph while at Project Vote. True power, he came to learn, was to master the principles of political marketing, and that led to vote getting. He applied these principles and was elected to the post of State Senator. Six years later he became U.S. Senator. No longer did he simply glimpse at power; he now saw the elegance and beauty of it. His unadulterated vision to raise the poor from poverty was well within his grasp. He was relentless. Soon his appeal attracted thirty thousand more volunteers to knock on doors to garner votes across the country. Foot soldiers scoured urban neighborhoods and once they secured those votes they canvassed the suburbs of the middle class and wealthy. The message these volunteers delivered was music to everyone's ears. *Change is coming! Yes we can! Transparency in government!* As his power grew with the middle class and the poor, a more dominant marketing force emerged—the Internet—which O'Boyle mastered and used to raise more money and votes than any other candidate in the history of politics.

"It all started with a young boy and his dream. Unlike so many of us, he never forgot or stopped believing in that dream. His boyhood vision never left him. Listen to his campaign speeches. It's clear he's never lost his beliefs in creating a just society for the poor and downtrodden, and leveling the playing field so everyone receives an equal chance. Today, the poor still have not been raised out of poverty; they remain disenfranchised. The only way to franchise them, according to O'Boyle, is to redistribute the wealth in this nation.

"Redistribution of wealth means different things to different people. For purposes of our discussion, it means to equate social democracy. I cannot draw a roadmap of what America will look like after O'Boyle completes his vision for the poor, but the new society will be a social democracy, the type which exists, for example, in Denmark, Finland, the Netherlands, Norway and Sweden. In governments such as these, considerable resources are spent on the poor to guarantee them good housing, food, free healthcare and education for all. Given are all the necessities of life, and gained is the virtue that society has helped the poor to become model citizens.

"Redistribution of wealth had been criticized as well. Many people believe it's a financial drain on a nation to support a class of people who contribute little to their own welfare, and little to the country, for that matter. Others aim their criticism at the government for taxing its citizens at an inordinate rate. They hold the belief that no government has the right to appropriate earned wealth from the middle class, the wealthy, or private sector business, and then hand it over to the less fortunate, or, as some label them, the less deserving. The belief within this group is that each individual seeks their own level in life, and the government has no right to punish the majority of citizens in defense of the few. Social democracy also begs the question why any business person would spend a lifetime building a business, undertake the associated financial risks, and deal with the day-to-day stress, only to have to hand over their acquired wealth to others because some leader wants to fulfill his vision for the poor.

"Whether you agree with redistribution of wealth or not, it is destined to become the fate of America. O'Boylecare was the first step toward social democracy. The next step, which has already begun, is the gradual escalation of taxes on the middle class, the wealthy and corporations. The president has targeted big business in particular as the prime source of revenue to fulfill his vision of a social democratic government in America.

"The event: You have now heard all three elements that make up this event. Recall, the first element is the fact that, since the turn of the century, the president and Congress have shown their inability to curtail spending of taxpayer money. Their negligence has reduced our once-great nation to nothing but a debt-ridden country. Second: we are in a civil war where the balance of power will soon be tipped in favor of one political party over the other. Voters of the dominant party will have the power to elect their candidates into office with little or no challenge from the opposing party. And third: the president's vision for this nation is to raise the poor out of poverty, something that will be accomplished by wealth redistribution. Said differently, our capitalist society will be transformed into a social democracy. The event has begun and no impediment will derail the president from achieving his goal. He controls the popular vote, will soon control both houses of Congress, and only an act of God could hamper him from carrying out his vision.

"It would take a decade or more to redistribute America's wealth," Charlie said.

"O'Boyle's party already has a majority in the Senate, and the mid-term elections are coming up. If he can win the majority of seats in the House, he'll then be able to pass new laws that will lead to the redistribution of wealth.

"The machinery is already in place for O'Boyle to influence voters, raise money, and to maintain his power on the path to social democracy. The incorporation of O'Boyle's non-profit organization, Organizing for Action, took place in 2012. It was financed with $5 million in leftover campaign contributions. No one gave this non-profit company much thought at the time, but it employs an analytics force of some of the best behavioral scientists, data technologists and mathematicians in the country.

"These brilliant individuals worked tirelessly to get O'Boyle reelected using a marketing strategy called microtargeting. Here's how it works. Background information is collected on every American citizen and entered into a computer database. Information such as voter history, gender, income bracket, demographics, personal preferences, likes and dislikes, newspapers read, websites visited, and just about every pertinent piece of information that can be collected on each and every American citizen is compiled. They then write programs to take this database of information and create a profile on each individual, how each person thinks, how they react to a new stimuli, new situations, and how they are likely to vote on any issue or topic presented to them. They pay less attention to those who already support O'Boyle. But greater care is taken with those who oppose him or who are on the fence, such as independent voters. They then develop tailor-made messages based on the voter's profile. The messages, some subliminal and some not, have the sole purpose of convincing these voters that O'Boyle shares their values on practically every issue. Eventually these messages will affect the voter's behavior. As the messages are delivered over and over again, you'll see that the ones relating to sensitive topics, such as *redistribution of wealth*, will eventually become innocuous to the voter's ear. That is how, over time, O'Boyle will create an even larger group of loyal supporters. Never before has there been a more powerful and persuasive marketing strategy to change the behavior of the American public. And the technology that performs this change in behavior belongs to neither political party; it is owned outright by Backer O'Boyle."

"O'Boyle will leave office one day. How does he maintain his power?"

"He will select his predecessor before he leaves office. He has already decided to throw his support behind H. McClinton, since she is the most popular candidate in his party. She must, though, agree to continue his work and his vision, and pledge to continue his goal to uplift the poor in a society that has failed to do so. Over the next decade or two, gradual tax increases will achieve wealth redistribution to the poor. Financial support, possibly in the trillions of dollars, will be deposited into programs that will pass unimpeded to this group. The transition will be achieved subtly and covertly, and completed long before middle-class Americans realize they are being taxed at a fifty-five percent rate. Corporations and the wealthy will be taxed at a seventy percent rate. These are the same tax rates levied on citizens in Sweden, Denmark and other social democratic countries.

"Now, if H. McClinton tells O'Boyle that she will not go along with his social democratic plan, he will pass her over and install Joe Burden as our next president. What gives O'Boyle the power to become kingmaker? Well, Organizing for America allows him to deliver fifty-three percent of the popular vote. That alone will be enough to elect the next president. Never in the history of this country has any one person wielded the power that Backer O'Boyle will wield over the next twenty-five years."

"What happens when voters find out O'Boyle's plan is to transform America into a social democracy?" Robert asked.

"O'Boyle will never speak those words or tip his hand of his deepest desire. Good politicians eliminate words that frighten people."

"How does the Fortune 500 see it?" Delsi said.

"Corporations believe they are the cow to be milked dry of their profits, and it will be their hard-earned income that turns America into a social democracy. Once they leave, they'll save trillions in taxes and get out from the burden of this country's national debt." Reny paused. "I cannot be more emphatic. Capitalism is not dead and the people of this world should not hate it. The U.S. was the last great bastion for capitalism, but O'Boyle and his supporters want to destroy it. So, the time has come to part ways. Capitalism will build its own nation and survive."

"Isn't there something we can do to stop them?"

"Can you stop a dam from flooding the countryside once it's burst? An event is final. It cannot be undone. When it strikes, it will be in the blink of an eye. O'Boyle has allowed Americans to believe that capitalism is evil and divisive. At this point, all capitalism can do is find a safe haven where it can flourish. To remain here is to be drained of all profit and thrown on the roadside like carrion." Reny looked at Charlie, Robert and Delsi. "This concludes my presentation."

Robert raised his hand. "What I take away from everything you've said is that we have a president who's trying to improve the condition of the people. As for myself, I've already stated that big business is corrupt, and it demeans the individual. In that regard, I see nothing wrong with using the principles of social democracy to improve the conditions of the middle class and the poor. When I stop to think about it, I still can't get my head around the fact that so many poor people in the richest country of the world still don't have the necessities of daily life. I'm talking about decent housing, food, and quality education." He paused briefly. "Another thing, not everyone born into this world wants to be a capitalist or entrepreneur. Why do we put so much pressure on people when most individuals only want to live a simple peaceful life? Where is it written that we have to work ourselves to the bone and make money? Capitalism is fair only to those on top, like the *banksters* who concoct financial schemes that put tens of millions of people out of work. They destroy everything in their path, while a society based on social democracy will create a level playing field where all Americans can share in the fruits of their labor."

Charlie looked at Delsi. "I'm sure you have something to say."

"I've been listening to people get on their soap boxes and disparage this country for its treatment of the poor since I was a little girl. The U.S. does more for poor people than any other country in the world, yet all we hear from the poor and bleeding hearts like Robert is how these people are kept down and prevented from living the American dream. Cruelty and injustice exists in this world, yes, but since 1964 this country has spent over $2 trillion in programs to raise the poor out of poverty. There are no more programs to offer them—we've tried them all. Drive through poor neighborhoods at night and you see gangs of kids standing on street corners. Why aren't they home doing their homework? Where are their parents? How can you blame good teachers for not wanting to teach in schools where kids don't care about education, about themselves or their future? The cycle of poverty will not be broken until people take responsibility for their own lives and stop blaming others for their social condition.

"To listen to Robert, social democracy is the cure-all for every ill that plagues this country. Well, I've got news for you Robert. Chavez instituted social democracy in Venezuela twelve years ago. The poor of the country were given decent housing, food, and free education for their children. At the same time, the murder and crime rate has risen over forty percent. You can't just give people things and expect them to become model citizens. The more you give, the more they complain that they're shortchanged, and the more they want. Venezuela, a country with oil reserves larger than those in Iran, Russia and Saudi Arabia combined, is now in debt for trillions of dollars because of their socialist spending to raise the poor out of poverty. Is this what you want for the United States?

"I would also like to remind Robert that our Constitution states that we live in a democratic republic, not a socialist nation. Our boys fought two world wars to protect the liberty and freedom as defined by our Constitution. They fought in places that had names they couldn't even pronounce. They fought for the American dream, and for the belief that every person is free to go after whatever they want in life. Our boys fought for that right, Robert, to allow freedom to reign forever in this land. American blood soaks the soil of every distant continent, and these soldiers did not sacrifice their blood so some politician could strip liberty out from under us, bury us in taxes, and usurp the meaning of our Constitution with his own distorted vision. I'd like to hear what those boys buried in Flanders Field and Normandy would think about your social democracy."

The fire in Delsi's eyes raged. Reny waited for her to cool down before speaking. Looking at Charlie, he said, "I have asked someone else to speak with you. Can you come back tomorrow? It will only take an hour or so."

"Who is this person?"

"A man with a slightly different perspective. I think you and your team will find what he says interesting."

Charlie looked at Robert and Delsi. "Okay. We'll come back in the morning."

"Good." Reny picked up his laptop and motioned for Charlie to join him in the hallway. He held an envelope in his hand. "If you decide to negotiate the deal with Canada for us, and if the Prime Minister agrees to accept the Fortune 500's offer, open this letter before you agree to any terms with him. If you decide not to negotiate the deal, destroy it."

"I understand." Charlie took the letter and returned to the conference room with Delsi and Robert. "What do you think about his presentation?"

"It's hard to believe everything he's told us," Delsi said. "It doesn't seem possible this could happen to America. Yet, I've had a strange feeling for a long time that this country was changing, and not for the better. "

"Maybe it is for the better," Robert said. "People will accept only so much suffering before they rise up and over-throw their oppressor."

"As for me," Charlie said. "I didn't realize the gravity of what I was getting myself into, or dragging you two into. I feel like a traitor taking on this project, and yet, if I stay involved maybe I can find a way to turn things around, or at least salvage some good out of it."

"Like what?" Delsi said.

"I don't know. All I can hope for is to recognize it when I see it."

"I hate to admit this," Robert said. "But some things Reny said are correct. The president *is* targeting the Fortune

500. I know this because I ran into a colleague of mine the other night who was recently out with Joe Burden and a couple of senators. After a couple of drinks, Burden said the only way to pay down our debt is to tax the hell out of Wall Street and the private sector, and that's exactly what Backer and he plan to do, he said."

"And you don't see anything wrong with that?" Delsi said.

"We're all going to get nailed with higher taxes, but for some reason it appears the president has a vendetta against big business. I don't know why. Maybe someday we'll find out." Robert looked at his watch. "I have an appointment uptown. I'll check in with you two later."

After Robert left, Delsi thought it was a good time to have a heart-to-heart with Charlie. "You've been very quiet lately. Is everything all right?"

"I'm fine. First I was exhausted from the campaign trail and, just as I was about to snap out of it, well, Angela's leaving has kept me in a funk. A month on a tropical island would do the trick, although, maybe not. It was lonely those couple of days I was in Acapulco without Angela."

"Where do things stand right now?"

"It's amicable. I know she loves me, but she needs time for herself. I just don't know how long that'll take. For now though, I'm grateful that we're seeing each other."

"If you don't mind me asking, are you up for negotiating this deal with Canada?"

Charlie ran his hands through his hair. "If I do, I just hope I don't lose Angela."

CHAPTER TWENTY

By the time he was eight years old, Backer O'Boyle had seen much more than most children his age. He knew the difference between being poor and living below the poverty line. He had never tasted poverty, mostly because his mother always managed to find work and put food on the table and clothes on his back. Life as a young boy was rocky for him; his mother moved them from place to place and even from country to country several times. His father had left when Backer was too young to remember him. The first time, his father moved to Boston to attend Harvard so he could get his doctorate degree. The next move was in response to a job offer in another country. There always seemed to be a reason to leave Backer and his mother behind. Years later Backer learned that his father had started another family and would never return.

Backer was a precocious child, and when, in sixth grade, other children pointed out that he was different, their words both angered and hurt him. When children are told they are different, they start to believe it. If told often enough, it eventually creates a scar that can never be removed, one that is indelibly scorched into the heart. Backer did not want to be different, and it pained him to see other children tortured in the same way. If he could gather them all in his arms and comfort them, he would.

At age twelve, Backer travelled to one country in particular where he saw poverty firsthand. He heard the horrible sound of a baby crying from hunger and learned that the human stomach feeds on itself from the inside out—a lesson that remained etched in his mind forever. Even as a young man, Backer thought God must love certain people more than all others because He placed such a heavy burden on their shoulders. Backer knew God would not do that unless He thought they were strong enough to support such weight. When the starving baby finally died, blinding tears filled Backer's eyes. So moved was Backer that he walked to a nearby tree and hugged it. He looked up with eyes that pleaded, "Please God, lift the weight from the children and place it on me."

CHAPTER TWENTY-ONE

Angela let Charlie into her apartment, shut the door and turned to him. "Are you going to tell me your secret now or do we have to play twenty questions?"

More than anything Charlie wanted to tell Angela what he was involved with, but he had signed a non-disclosure agreement, so telling her was not an option. And, he had not yet committed himself one way or the other. He still had twenty-three hours to make up his mind. "If you asked a thousand questions you'd never guess what's going on."

"Nothing changes, does it, Charlie. Always a big deal brewing somewhere, and you're right in the middle of it. We've been down this road before, but I'm not doing it this time.

"Angela, I—"

"Don't make excuses, Charlie. If you want a life with me, you need to make a choice."

"Angela, this is something big. Right now I'm just not in a position to walk away from it."

"Tell me what it is, then."

Charlie sighed. "I signed an agreement and can't."

"We signed an agreement, too. We promised to love, honor and respect one another. Which agreement do you want, Charlie?"

"Angela, slow down a moment. I love you, and our agreement is more important. All I'm asking for is a bit of time to work through this matter. As soon as this is over we can settle down, just like you want, and I want, too."

Angela thought about it. "Will you have to travel?"

"If I do decide to take this on, yes, I'll be away. I don't want to mislead you. If I involve myself with this project, I may need to move to Canada for a while. If I do, I want you and Kaitlin to come with me."

Angela shook her head in disbelief. "And just like that my career stops again. Go on. Say it! Tell me to quit my show!"

"Don't put words in my mouth."

"It's not fair. I'm not a human being to you. I have no freedom, no right in any decisions. No Charlie, I won't throw my life away only to have to rebuild it yet again." She turned her back to him. "It's broken Charlie, and I'm scared we can't fix it. It's better if you leave now."

* * *

Michael Reny was alone in his hotel room when someone knocked on his door. When he opened it, Delsi was standing in the hallway. He stepped aside and allowed her to enter. "You have another model for me to look at?" he asked.

"No, I have no models to show you." She stood close to him. "I'm not very good at expressing matters that concern my heart. I have a horrible sense of timing as well as a proclivity to be painfully direct, even when my comments may embarrass those hearing them, and me, as well." She paused a moment and searched his face. "To me, you're an incredible man, but intensely lonely, as though exiled on some remote island. You're incredible because your insights go beyond what most see, and to twist even the smallest fact to your advantage is not within you. I doubt there is anyone else in this world quite like you." She inched closer. "I have never said 'I love you' to a man. I never knew the meaning of those words or how they're supposed to make you feel inside. When I look at you, though, a feeling runs through my body like none I've ever known. I think I can truthfully say that what I feel is love. Yes, it is. I love you, Michael. I want to believe I can say those words just once in my life and have it last forever. To expect a man to speak those words to me and mean it forever might be naïve, but I want to believe it can happen." Delsi took a deep breath. "I'm going to leave now, but before I go I have one more thing to say." She placed her hand gently on his cheek and kissed his lips. She stepped away and looked into his eyes, and then turned and left his room.

* * *

Yuri Kosyachenko walked into the conference room at exactly 7:30 a.m. He bowed slightly to everyone before removing his hat and coat. "Good morning," he said with a deep Russian accent. "Michael asked I come speak with you." He was short and wide, with thinning, silver hair and the typical Slavic ski-slope nose. His eyes smiled as he looked around the room. "I am former KGB agent. In 1987, I defect to Canada. In those days Kremlin have thousand spies in U.S.A. My assignment was 1960 where my team was to demoralize Western values. What values are these? In those days, cold war days, U.S.A. gave hope to world. Opportunity, freedom, to live in great country and not fear government take your home, your land, or put you in camp and never see your family again. Russia never compete well against such things. So slowly we infiltrate to change culture. To brainwash takes decades, and we began fifty years ago to change meaning of democracy in minds of people. Slowly at first, and over time democracy began to mean different thing to most Americans. By 1980, Russia no longer needed so many agents in U.S.A. because Americans began to demoralize themselves. Country went from nationalism to such open-minded society that no two people believe in same thing about country. This is crisis stage, followed by current stage of civil war. What you call 'conquer and divide,' and right out of Russian manual on how to defeat enemy from within.

"I am old man and have seen much. I work in Politburo, Siberia and Russian gulags where penal colony are many. I have seen death camps that world still know nothing about, where Stalin, just one man, make millions of innocent comrades disappear. Children dumped in pile like garbage and burned into ashes. Year after year Stalin scoop up village of people and accuse simple man enemy to Communism. The bloodshed, terror, ignoble treatment, all so evil and with no justification for so many dead. Then, extermination go beyond murder of peasants. Soon officials from Politburo disappear. Bourgeoisie friends of Stalin disappear. Even KGB disappear in night. I defect to protect my family.

"The U.S.A. at one time greatest country in world. Now you lost your way. Look at people in country. Many so ignorant it disgraces nation. I bet my friend Alexander Krivitsky one hundred dollars that no American can explain the word *Republic* written in U.S.A. Constitution. So we walk down avenue and ask young people. No one can answer question. I then ask what is American Constitution? Still no one explain. How is possible that greatest country have citizens like this? In Russia all children know constitution, know history, know presidents. In America each person have own idea of right and wrong, good and bad, even president. Each group of people hate or fear other group. Now we call America nation of islands of people. Russia could not achieve so much subversion in one hundred years.

"I live in Welland and watch big ships come through canal. It good place to live. People know constitution and history. This why I defect here. But U.S.A. remind me of Bolshevik revolution. The poor so angry, rich not share, and leader blind by own vision and not see country dying around him. Putin sit back with bag of popcorn and watch on large screen TV. He has smile on face for soon collapse of America happen. Moral decay everywhere in country. How is possible seventy percent babies from wedlock by some? And government finance this living for people? Prisons ten times more people than decade ago. Young people no respect for country. In inauguration speech President tell people country is unfair, must free poor from bondage. People must take to street in civil disobedience as only way for more just, more equal, more free, more caring America."

"Excuse me, Yuri," Robert said. Are you certain Backer O'Boyle said that in his inauguration speech?"

"2008 speech. I have hundred dollar in pocket. We bet first, then look on Internet?"

"No, that's all right. I'm not a betting man."

"Confusion. How can U.S.A. be great when president speech send such message to citizens? How citizens feel good about hard work done to build country? Was poor who built U.S.A.? He confuse hard-working people, and Putin have smile on face and eat popcorn and wait. Subversion by Russia never equal America subversion to own people."

"Do you have a point to all this?" Charlie asked.

"Sorry my English not so good. You now see America like foreigner see country. I mention evil of Russia so you see how possible one man change world. Stalin know how to divide and conquer his people, like many leader in history. First they strip dignity, and next freedom. America have best freedom in history, but Fortune 500 will leave and freedom may be taken too. I, Yuri Kosyachenko, see America with open eyes, with no brainwashing, no hate for one faction over other. I say, do not allow anyone to replace freedom for socialism. Hold freedom close to your heart. Smell it like sweet nectar, taste it each single day. Once it gone you never have it again. Only strong leader can help America now, with words not to divide country, but to unite people. This is only hope for America.

"Now, this thing called socialism. You been told lie. If people accept socialism then you live in controlled world where government tells people how to exist, what to eat, how to breathe, how to think, and how to die. I am old man and see world change many times. Funny Russia now is capitalistic and America like Bolsheviks, where poor only want to destroy rich, and will even take middle class, their homes, all possessions. Envy and hate stronger in America than any country. Socialism not change those people who kill all but own kind. As society decays it is nature of people to care only for their kind. And government no better. They tell poor today they are cheated by other citizens, but soon will be elevated to level playing field. Soon their dream come true when all people equal. What does that mean? Nothing. Just words. Where in history has such thing happened? How can each man not know he must fight and make his own world? Freedom allowed in America for such thing. Politician say to poor they will be equal soon. Good way to get votes. I say to men, go forth in such a great nation and make your destiny true. In 1917 Bolsheviks try to make people equal in Russia. For decades they believed it, and U.S.S.R. collapse in 1991. America to die if travels this dark road. Freedom will die, and in hundred years young Russian boys and girls will read about empire, the U.S.A. that had all, but leader confuse people, like Stalin in Russia many years ago. He convince proletariat those millions of murdered people were enemies of state. Good way to divide and conquer. His words soothe them, persuade them that he tell truth. Luminous are men who have such skill and then take nations over. In blink of eye all is lost. Do not fall asleep America, is what I say. You throw most valuable thing away. Your freedom. That is all I say to you." Yuri put on his coat and hat. As he walked to the door he waved goodbye and was gone.

CHAPTER TWENTY-TWO

Max Plummer's jet landed at Ottawa Airport just as the snow let up. Max allowed Charlie use of the jet for his trip to meet with the Prime Minister of Canada. Charlie, Robert and Delsi disembarked from the jet and were greeted by an awaiting limousine that drove them to Gatineau Park, the residence of Prime Minister Stephen Harper. Max knew the prime minister from past oil leasing deals and had made arrangements for Charlie and his team to meet with him. Given the delicate nature of the subject matter they need-ed to discuss, the prime minister suggested they meet at his residence.

Delsi and Robert had worked diligently to prepare the presentation. They both agreed there was nothing to gain by delivering a prolonged speech to the prime minister, and that the best approach was to lay their cards on the table and tell him they were interested in buying two of Canada's provinces.

"...and for Manitoba and Saskatchewan, Mr. Prime Minister, we're prepared to pay off Canada's national debt of $1.1 trillion. In addition, I hold in my hand a check made out to the Government of Canada in the amount of $7.9

trillion. Canada retains all oil and mineral rights in both provinces and agreements with the Cree and other indigenous peoples in the provinces will be upheld. All Canadians living within the borders of the provinces will retain full legal right to their property and, of course, remain Canadian citizens if that is their preference."

Prime Minister Harper did not take his eyes off Charlie the entire time he was speaking. The prime minister stared at the document Charlie had placed before him. He read it over with care. Finally, he came to the last two pages which listed the signatures of three hundred and eighty-five Fortune 500 CEOs. After examining the document in its entirety, the prime minister stood up and walked to the window, where he placed both hands behind his back and gently rocked back and forth on his heels. "I don't believe I've ever heard a more unusual offer in my lifetime."

"Yes, we understand, sir."

"Have you a name for this new country?"

"That hasn't been decided, sir. Our present mission is to ascertain whether Canada will entertain such an offer at this time."

"I see. And what about all the hardworking people this 'arrangement' will leave behind?"

"We plan to bring them, sir."

"How many will come?"

"Initially, five million."

"In total?"

Charlie looked at Robert and Delsi. "In time, thirty-five million. But possibly a great many more, sir."

The prime minister turned and looked at Charlie. His expression did not change. "I imagine these are people who can contribute."

"That's correct, sir."

The prime minister looked out the window once again and, after deliberating a moment longer, he walked back and joined his guests at the table. "I don't know how to react to what you've just proposed. Nor do I know how to articulate such an offer to Parliament."

"We understand your dilemma, sir."

"Selling off a part of Canada...I'm not sure about that, and I have no idea how Parliament will react to such an offer. I will speak with a few key members and get their thoughts before I convene with Parliament in two days from now. I can only promise to have your offer added to my calendar that day, nothing more. It will certainly get the juices flowing on both sides of the aisle."

"We're prepared to remain in Canada for the duration, sir."

"That might be wise. I imagine there will be plenty of questions to answer."

They sat at the table just a minute more until Charlie realized everything that needed to be said had been said. "All right, sir. You have our contact information. We'll wait to hear from you." They stood up, shook hands with the prime minister, and left his residence.

* * *

The jet was at Charlie's disposal. With time to spare, he asked the pilot to fly them over Saskatoon, just one area of Canada the Fortune 500 hoped to purchase. Saskatoon is the largest city in Saskatchewan with a population of 252,000. From their seats in the jet, the countryside was beautiful to view. Saskatchewan was bound on the west by Alberta, the east by Manitoba, the north by the Northwest Territories, and to the south by North Dakota and Montana. The three passengers decided a tour guide would be helpful as they flew over the province. The pilot called down to request one, and within minutes he landed the jet in Saskatoon to pick one up. The jet was just as quickly airborne once again. They flew over Cypress Hills in the southwestern part of Saskatchewan, then over Killdeer Badlands, and then over the National Grasslands, all areas untouched by the last glaciation period. The guide pointed out all fourteen major drainage basins, where they saw water that emptied into both the Arctic Ocean and the Hudson Bay. Incredibly, some Canadian water eventually reaches the Gulf of Mexico. The jet landed again, this time outside the city of Moose Jaw. From there they drove to Swift Current, a smaller city of 15,000 residents. They saw the oldest-operating business in town, the Imperial Hotel, which was built in 1903.

Robert and Delsi were anxious to try the local fare, so the guide took them to a restaurant known for its trout sandwiches. Charlie wasn't hungry. Instead, he decided to explore this part of the province on his own. He drove the car to the outskirts of the city which, to his eyes, was pure wilderness. He stepped out of the car to take it all in. Yellow primroses sprang from rock crevices, and foot-high elephant heads bloomed with bright pink and purple flowers. Goldenrod sprouted from the earth far and wide, and grass types were too numerous to count. In the distance, waves of wheat swayed in the field as far as the eye could see. In the solitude of the moment, Charlie began to whistle "America the Beautiful." A fine rain began to mist the air. Moments later it came down in sheets and forced him back to the car. He opened the door and, before stepping inside, looked back at the massive, beautiful land and tried to envision office buildings and subdivisions where wheat swayed across the endless plains.

CHAPTER TWENTY-THREE

The office building did not need to be cleaned on the weekend, and it allowed Delilah to spend more time with Ronnie. It also allowed her to retire earlier and catch up on her much needed rest. While asleep that Saturday night she was awakened by a knock on the front door. The clock next to the bed indicated one a.m. She looked at Ronnie, who was sound asleep. Delilah got out of bed and went into the outer room. She saw Mama was still asleep on the couch. Delilah pulled the curtain back to peek out and see who was at her door. Kenny was standing there. She opened the door a crack.

"Whatcha want, Kenny? You ain't s'pose to be here." By the look in his eyes she knew he'd been drinking. His face had a sly smile on it. "Go on now," she said, pushing the door closed. Kenny wedged his foot in the doorway.

"Why you bein' so beeechy?" he said. He buckled and laughed. "You were a celebrity a while back, Delilah. They were all tweetin' at ya then." He pushed his way through the door and into the house. Delilah backed up into the room.

"Gonna call the police, Kenny."

"Come now, Delilah. It's me. You remember what it's like. Don't tell me different."

Delilah backed up even more as Kenny walked toward her. Any further and she'd end up in the bedroom where Ronnie was sleeping. Kenny put his arms around her. He kissed her face and groped her. She pulled away; the smell of alcohol sickened her. By now Mama was awake. She got off the couch and went straight to where Kenny and Delilah were standing.

"Take your hands off her."

Kenny had a smile on his face, but it disappeared. "Woman, I'll crack you." He raised his open hand, but Mama did not back away. It had been a long time, but she knew the feeling of being hit by a man, and she was not afraid. No one was going to put his hand on her baby girl.

"Don't you touch my mama."

Kenny turned to Delilah in anger. No one told him what to do. His hand clenched into a fist and he struck her in the face. Delilah fell to the floor.

Delilah looked up, momentarily dazed. "They goin' lock you up for that."

"You think you somethin', don't you," he said. "Samuel L. Axon didn't call it right when talkin' 'bout you. You ain't no craaazy beeech; you a fat craaazy beeech."

It had been two months since Samuel L. made that tweet about her, and it was still being thrown in her face.

Kenny laughed at his comment and then looked toward the kitchen. He walked in and opened the cupboard door and looked up at the crock pot. "See you still keep it here." He took the lid off and began stuffing his pockets.

Delilah was still on the floor holding her face. "Don't take it, Kenny. That Ronnie's college money."

Kenny laughed. "You crazy girl. You think that boy goin' to college?"

"Don't take it. I'll do whatcha want."

Kenny walked past her and out the door. Mama helped Delilah to her feet. When she got her balance, she saw Ronnie watching from the bedroom door.

* * *

Delilah kept her head down. When customers thanked her for bagging their groceries, she said "You're welcome" but resisted looking anyone in the eye. Kenny's hit had left her face half-swollen, and her left eye was bruised and closed. Twice the store manager passed by her, and twice she turned away from him. The cashier caught a glimpse of Delilah's face. "What happened?" The manager overheard and walked over.

"I need to speak to you, Delilah."

Delilah finished bagging the customer's groceries and walked into the back room where the store manager was waiting.

"What happened to you, Delilah?"

"I was cleaning last night and slipped and hit the corner of the coffee table. It'll clear up soon."

"Delilah, I can't have you bagging groceries. Customers are funny about their food being handled by someone who's hurt."

"No one's seen it. I keep my head down."

"I'm sorry, Delilah. You can't work on the floor looking like that."

"How 'bout back here, breakin' an' tyin' boxes?"

"They're all broke and tied already. I'm afraid you'll have to go home. Don't worry. You're not fired. I'll put you back on the schedule as soon as the swelling and bruises are gone."

"Yes, sir. Thanks for lettin' me come back. I need this job."

"Okay. Take care of yourself and call me when you're better.

Delilah put on her coat and left through the back door of the store. The bus arrived not long after. All the way home she relived the moment Kenny had knocked her to the ground and stolen Ronnie's college money. What was worse, Ronnie had watched the whole thing from the bedroom doorway. After Kenny had left she called 911. A police car showed up twenty minutes later. Delilah told the police what had happened, and they immediately issued a warrant for Kenny's arrest.

Delilah's mind wandered back to the good old days when she was a princess in Kenny's eyes and when Ronnie had a caring father. The drugs had changed it all. They destroyed her marriage, and left her without a husband and Ronnie without a father. She then recalled the essay Ronnie had written about her, and the warmth of that thought allowed her to push Kenny out of her mind. It was the first time Ronnie had expressed his feelings for her in writing. A smile crossed her face as she repeated the words over and over to herself: *My mom is the greatest person in the world, and I love her because she takes good care of me.*

Delilah checked her watch. She would be home early enough to catch a nap before leaving for her second job. She stepped off the bus and walked down the avenue until she reached her street. When she turned onto her block, she saw a police car parked in front of her house. A policeman was trying to lift a woman to her feet, but the woman resisted him. She screamed and Delilah realized it was her mama on her knees in front of the policeman. She ran over to where the two were still on the sidewalk.

"Mama! What is it?"

"You baby, you Ronnie. He gone! He gone!"

CHAPTER TWENTY-FOUR

Backer O'Boyle was excited when his mother told him the news. His father was traveling halfway around the world just to visit him. Now ten, Backer had imagined what his father looked like. The tall, regal-looking man who stepped into their house did not look anything like Backer had envisioned.

He placed his hands on Backer's shoulders and introduced himself as Backer's father. Backer stiffened, not knowing how to respond in this man's presence. It was his father, but Backer did not know him. He stayed two weeks. By the time he left, Backer had fallen in love with him. After all, what boy does not want a father? One night Backer lay wide awake in bed trying to think of a way to ask him to stay. The next morning, however, his father left and Backer never saw him again.

Years later, Backer received a telephone call from a distant country. The person at the other end of the phone told him his father had been killed. Gone was Backer's imaginary world in which only he and his father existed. His father had been his lifeline so many times and in so many ways, even though his father's help only existed in Backer's imagination.

Backer travelled to the faraway land to learn about the father he never really knew. Backer learned that his father once had a well-paying position at a large oil company. But he was an academic, an idealist, a man with high principles, and sometimes officious, all qualities that rarely meld well in the dog-eat-dog business world. Backer was unable to determine if his father was asked to leave the company or if he left on his own volition. From there, Backer learned, his father had taken on a job working for the government in the country where he lived. Life did not get better for him and slowly his existence took a downward spiral.

After learning all he needed to learn about his father, Backer returned home. One night, his father came to him in a dream. He apologized for not being a better father and for not giving as all fathers should. He told Backer that, in the ten-year-old boy he had met, he had seen great wisdom and intelligence. He was sorry he had never said that to him, but he wanted to say it now. *Use what you've been given to make this world a better place.* In the mirror the next morning, Backer noticed dried tears on his cheeks. He remembered his father's visit from the night before. Looking into the mirror once more, he promised himself he *would* make the world a better place.

CHAPTER TWENTY-FIVE

Robert caught a taxi into the city after leaving LaGuardia Airport. He, Charlie and Delsi had remained in Ottawa for four days. At one point they met with Parliament in a closed session for over eight hours, answering question after question about their proposed purchase. All three were completely spent. After four exhausting days together, they needed a break from each other. They welcomed the opportunity to take separate taxis back to the city.

Robert bought a copy of The New York Times to read on the ride home. Page one had an article about several growing right-wing movements in Europe: young Hungarian men tormenting gypsies, English skinheads protesting the building of mosques in their neighborhood, and gangs of Germans outraged by the increase of foreigners in their country. The article mentioned dozens of other countries with similar social issues. It occurred to Robert that the Fortune 500 may also run into some form of bias in their move to Canada. Many Americans consider Canada a good place for a summer home or as an occasional vacation spot, but rarely do they take Canada seriously. As a result, there is no love lost for the United States on the part of many Canadians. Some

Americans even think Canada should be grateful to have the U.S. as their neighbor. After all, who would dare to attack America's neighbor? What most Americans don't know is that Canada entered World War II in 1939, two full years before the United States decided to enter the fray. By the end of the War, Canada possessed the world's fourth largest air force and third largest navy. Quietly, they lost 45,000 men on foreign soil.

Robert flipped through the pages looking for other articles of interest. One in particular caught his eye.

Boy Killed Outside School Playground. Twelve-year-old Ronnie Jones was struck and killed by a car as he fled from a group of students during recess at Public School 19. Reporters questioned the teacher who had tried unsuccessfully to disband the students. She said the incident stemmed from a Twitter message sent about the upcoming presidential inauguration. The person who sent the Twitter message, name unknown, chastised Delilah Jones, mother of the victim, for voting for Matt Roman. During the school recess Samuel L. Axon replied to the Twitter message by saying that Delilah Jones must be in mourning over Matt Roman's loss to O'Boyle. It appears these were not the first Twitter messages posted about Mrs. Jones. Mr. Axon's fame and celebrity as an actor may have added credibility to his message. As a result, the students became overly excited by Axon's words. According to the teacher, the students surrounded Jones and chanted "Matt Roman. Your mama voted for Matt Roman." Jones became frightened. In his panic, the young boy ran from the playground to escape the other students. He darted into the street without looking, and an approaching car struck and killed him. The driver of the car was not charged. Calls made to Samuel L. Axon have not been returned.

Robert folded the newspaper and tossed it on the seat. How was it possible for this young boy to be dead because someone three thousand miles away typed a few words into his cell phone? And why was his mother being ridiculed for deciding to vote for one candidate over another? Something was terribly wrong with a society that mocks fellow men and women in this manner. He recalled Delsi's words from just a few days earlier: Soldiers have died to give each and every individual the right to vote their conscience. It's their inalienable right. How could anyone in America be scorned for exercising their most fundamental right? Had people respected that right, this young boy would be alive today.

The incident brought to mind Ralph Bunche. While in Canada, Robert had taken time to research Bunche as Delsi had instructed him to after one of their heated debates. Robert read everything he could find on the man. Ralph Bunche and his two sisters were orphaned when his mother died in 1917, and they were raised by their grandmother in Los Angeles. Ralph sold newspapers, worked as a houseboy, and found odd jobs—anything to bring additional money into the household. Rarely did a day go by that Ralph did not work at one job or another. In spite of that, he graduated valedictorian from high school. He received an athletic scholarship to U.C.L.A. The scholarship paid for his tuition only. He worked as a janitor to cover his personal expenses. And still, he graduated summa cum laude.

Ralph went on to teach at Howard, Harvard and many other universities. He excelled as a professor and his students loved and respected him. In their search for high-caliber men, the Truman Administration offered Ralph a position. He declined because remnants of Jim Crow still remained in Washington, D.C. and Ralph, although not hostile, opposed any institution or person who tolerated segregation in any form whatsoever. The United Nations went on to hire Ralph, and he soon became known as a man who got the job done. Several years later, Ralph's diplomatic expertise came to light when, in 1950, he won the Noble Peace Prize for negotiating a treaty between Israel and the Arab States. Ralph returned home to a ticker tape parade on Broadway. Los Angeles declared 'Ralph Bunche Day.' He went on to receive over thirty honorary degrees. As the years passed, Ralph was diagnosed with heart disease and diabetes, He resigned as the United Nations Under-Secretary-General on October 1, 1971. He died December 9 that same year.

Delsi had wanted Robert to uncover a specific phrase spoken by Ralph Bunche. He continued to pore over everything published about Bunche. It took time, but Robert finally located the four words: *With Freedom Comes Responsibility*. He thought long and hard about those words, and also about the people to whom they applied. By the time the taxi reached the Fifty-ninth Street Bridge, Robert couldn't think of a single person to whom those words did not apply—from the president to the man who picked up his garbage every week.

Ralph Bunche wanted every American to know that we have been given a great gift in this country, a gift as precious and fragile as a baby bird. If you squeeze it too hard, drop it, fail to feed or love it, the baby bird will die. Ronnie Jones was a baby bird who had panicked and fallen from his nest. While so many had contributed to his tragic outcome, no one had come forward to claim responsibility for the boy's death—not his teachers, not the students who bullied him, not their parents, and not the popular actor whose one Twitter comment had driven other young students into a frenzy. Now a young boy lay on a cold slab in a Brooklyn morgue.

Robert stopped playing the 'what if' game and looked within himself. He was no better. Delsi had often told him to stop the grand speeches and do something constructive. For once she was right. What could he point to that says he has made a difference? What had he done to improve the life of even one person? He reached over and picked up the newspaper. He turned to the article about the young boy who had lost his life. "Delilah Jones."

CHAPTER TWENTY-SIX

FOR IMMEDIATE RELEASE:

Proposed House Joint Resolution 15 Seeks to Repeal Twenty-second Amendment - January 5, 2013.

On January 4, 2013, H.J.Res. 15 was reintroduced in Congress by Representative José Serrano (D-NY15). The legislation proposes an amendment to the Constitution that would repeal the 22nd Amendment, thereby removing the limitation on the number of terms an individual can serve as President of the United States. The bill, which has been referred to committee, would allow President Backer O'Boyle to become the first president since Franklin D. Roosevelt to seek a third term.

Few in Congress expect the 22nd Amendment to be repealed. The opposition party laughed at the idea when informed that Representative Serrano had actually proposed the legislation, saying, "that Backer O'Boyle wants to become king is no surprise to us." They went on to say that to repeal the 22nd Amendment requires that it be passed by both houses of Congress and ratified by three-quarters of the State Legislatures.

At a recent White House press conference, Press Secretary J. Carnie was asked if the president would consider a third term if, in fact, the 22nd Amendment were repealed. Carnie responded by saying, "the president is much too busy juggling important matters to respond to such questions."

Many in Congress believe the 22nd Amendment should be repealed, as every year or two a bill is reintroduced by one party or the other to that end. Most political pundits agree that the amendment will remain part of the Constitution as a protective measure to keep one political party from wheeling too much leverage over the legislative process, and too much power over opposing parties.

CHAPTER TWENTY-SEVEN

On the taxi ride from the airport to his apartment Charlie began reviewing the notes he had taken during his meeting with the Canadian Parliament. He went over every detail with a fine-toothed comb. When he arrived home, a thought occurred to him, and he began to read between the lines. He picked up the telephone.

"Delsi, I'm glad you got home safely. Are you exhausted?"

"Thanks, yes. Why do you ask?"

"I need you to create two new models for me, and I need them first thing in the morning."

"You're beginning to sound like your old self, Charlie."

"Sorry to dump this on you last minute, but we need to stay prepared."

"What do you need?"

"One model that shows what Canada looks like if they sell us Manitoba and Saskatchewan, and a second model showing the economic impact on Canada if they strike a deal to absorb the Fortune 500."

"What's going on, Charlie?"

"I've been reading over their questions again and am coming to the conclusion they might make us a counter offer.

You can bet our friends up north are crunching a lot of numbers right now. How powerful do you think Canada would become if those three hundred eighty-five Fortune 500 companies who've signed on became Canadian companies?"

"What an intriguing thought. Okay, I've got the picture. I'll work on the models tonight and have something for you in the morning."

"Thanks, Delsi. Good night."

"Good night, Charlie."

* * *

A police detective had gone to Delilah's home and explained how Ronnie had died. That wasn't enough for Delilah; she needed to hear how it happened from the teacher on duty at the school playground.

Ronnie's teacher, Mrs. Phillips, led Delilah into an empty classroom with a table and chairs. "Have a seat, Ms. Jones. I can't express how deeply sorry I am. Ronnie was such a nice boy. He was above average in all his subjects, and I know it's because you spent a great deal of time with him. He knew right from wrong, too, and never got into trouble. Ronnie enjoyed school and he stood out more than most students here."

"Don't mean to cut you off, but what 'bout that day? Can ya tell me 'bout it?"

"I'm sorry. Of course. What occurred in the playground was horrible. I don't know how things got so out of control. I turned around for only a second, and when I looked back about thirty students had surrounded him. They just converged on Ronnie and began to taunt him. Who would think a Twitter message would have the impact to incite young kids to heckle another student like that? Well, it did, and Ronnie panicked and ran. It all happened so suddenly, there was no way for me to stop it. I've gone over it a hundred times in my head to think if there was something I could have done differently. I know this isn't helping you, but I don't know what else to say."

"Did you see him run?"

Mrs. Phillips dropped her head for a moment and then looked directly at Delilah. "I saw him run and I yelled for him to stop, but he never heard me. He was terrified. All he wanted to do was to get away from those kids. I was helpless to do anything but watch it happen."

Delilah opened her purse and took out a tissue. Her hand shook as she wiped a stream of tears from her cheek. "Ronnie was a good boy. A good boy."

Mrs. Phillips nodded and cried, too. After a minute, she placed her hand on Delilah's shoulder. There was nothing more she could say to help her.

Delilah looked up at her. "Do me somethin'?"

"Anything, Ms. Jones."

"Ronnie's essay. You let me have it?"

"Wait here." Mrs. Phillips went into her classroom and removed his essay from the stack piled on her desk. A moment later she walked back into the room. "Here it is. It's quite beautiful."

Delilah folded it and placed it in her purse. "Need to go now." She stood up, nodded to Mrs. Phillips and walked out of the room. When she reached the front door, she removed the essay from her purse and read it. Alone, her tears ran like a river. She placed it back in her purse and walked to the corner and waited for the bus. When she got on and sat down, she counted out one hundred and twelve dollars. Delilah got off the bus at Main Street and walked two blocks to Foot Locker.

"I need size nine Air Jordans."

* * *

Delilah got home and sat at the table with her head buried in her arms. Her mother gently rubbed her back, telling her the Lord had taken Ronnie to Heaven. He needed him there. The stabbing pain would not let go, and Delilah cried even more tears as her mother embraced her. There was a knock on the door. Delilah's mother answered it.

"Yes?"

"Is Delilah Jones at home?"

"You is?"

"My name is Robert Devins."

Confused, she turned to Delilah, who stood up and walked to the door. She did not recognize the man.

"I apologize for intruding. I read about your son and wanted to offer any assistance I could."

Delilah looked at him with skepticism. "Nothin' no one can do," she said. Her mother placed her arm around Delilah's shoulder.

Suddenly Robert felt awkward. He should never have interfered in their grief and suffering. Embarrassed, he wanted to turn and leave, but that would only embarrass him more. "May I come in for a moment?"

Delilah tried to understand why this man was on her porch. What possible interest could he have in her? She took one step back, enough to allow him to enter. Her mother closed the door and Delilah returned to the couch.

Robert walked to the coffee table. "No one ever expects such a horrible thing to happen to a child, and I can't begin to understand what you're going through. I know this can create a financial burden on families." Robert hesitated. "I…I would like to make sure your son receives the type of burial you want for him. Have you made any arrangements yet?"

Delilah looked up. "He lay in a cold morgue downtown."

"Oh. Is there family to help you?"

Delilah sat motionless, but her mother shook her head indicating they had no one.

"The church? Will they help you?"

Delilah wiped her nose. "The minister's a good man and he's out raising money. He said it might be best to cremate Ronnie 'cause bury 'em cost so much. My Ronnie should be buried like decent folks." Delilah dropped her head. "My baby still layin' there and I haf to do somethin'."

"Delilah, would you allow me…I mean…"

She looked up at him. Her eyes grew wide. "You a stranger. You never know'd my boy."

Robert walked around the table and sat next to her. "Let me help give Ronnie a proper burial."

Delilah's shoulders began to heave. "You'll help me git 'em out of that cold place?" Warm tears flowed down her cheek.

"My car's outside. Let's go make his arrangements."

CHAPTER TWENTY-EIGHT

Charlie waved Delsi into the conference room when she arrived at the office.

"Where's Robert?"

"It's just the two of us this morning. He had something to do," Charlie said. "How did you make out with those models?"

Delsi took a seat next to him and turned on her laptop. "They're both done." She accessed the program and waited for it to load. "The first model shows Canada selling us the provinces, and the second one shows what happens if the Fortune 500 become Canadian companies. I'll start with the first one. Canada's the second largest country in the world at 4 million square miles of real estate. Only Russia at 6.5 million is larger. Not that it matters, but the U.S. is third with 3.8, and China takes fourth place with 3.7 million square miles. If Canada agrees to sell the provinces they drop to the fourth largest with 3.5 million square miles of land. But, with a population of only 35 million people, there's plenty of land to go around.

"The U.S. has the largest gross domestic product at $16.5 trillion. If the Fortune 500 were to leave, it would decline to

$8.7 trillion, and fall to second place behind China's GDP of $11.3 trillion. In this scenario, Canada, which has the fourteenth largest GDP of $1.4 trillion would drop to $1.1 trillion, but would keep their ranking.

"Now, if the Fortune 500 become Canadian companies, Canada would then be ranked as the third largest-producing country in the world at $7.7 trillion. Based on my model Canada would surpass the U.S. in five years to become the second largest-producing country in the world. Rapid immigration by Americans during this timeframe will eventually give Canada the most productive workforce in the world. At that point they'll only allow the crème de la crème into their country.

"One other thing. I looked at Canada's ability to lodge Americans in the event there's a mass exodus out of the U.S. They would be able to accommodate 4.5 million Americans at one time. If an exodus were to occur, it must be well managed and thought-out ahead of time. As emigrants purchase or build homes, it will allow additional Americans to emigrate into Canada. Let me get back to the models.

"With option two, where the Fortune 500 relocates to Canada, per capita it will become the wealthiest country in the world. It will be virtually debt fee, and within fifteen years Canada will surpass China with a GDP of $21 trillion. It will also become attractive to thousands of foreign corporations looking to expand their global presence, and many will consider relocating to Canada because it will have the most explosive economy in the world. Canada will also attract the best-educated and most talented workers from around the world. And with the second largest land mass in the world, there is no physical limitation for growth. The U.S. will see a significant amount of productive workers move to Canada because its economy will flourish, and within twenty years the Canadian population can reach 90 million citizens. If Americans continue to migrate out of the country, in fifty years Canada will surpass the population of the U.S.

"Canada takes their finances seriously. Those in power, whether conservative or liberal, understand the curse of over-spending and the importance of not becoming a debt-ridden economy. The Canadians will also have the luxury to cur-tail the influx of poorly educated and untrained immigrants, which will limit the cost of entitlements, welfare, food stamps and other safety-net expenses. Another interesting event will occur: Canada will have the muscle to kick the United States around, if they so desire. Canada will also need to provide financial assistance to the U.S. over the next decade in order to keep Russia and China away from their own border. On an earlier model that showed the collapse of the U.S. econo-my, I forecasted China or Russia as purchasing Alaska. But I see now that Canada has to make that purchase to protect itself from those two superpowers getting their hooks into North America.

"As for the U.S., all it will take for the economy to col-lapse is for two hundred and fifty corporations to leave. I ran this model again hoping for different results, but the out-come is the same. Inflation will make it impossible for people to put food on their table or to buy gas at a reasonable price. Chaos will rule the country, and to predict exactly what will occur at that point is difficult to foresee." Delsi saw the look on Charlie's face and decided to end her presentation. "Sorry,

I get carried away sometimes. Have you come up with any ideas on how to keep them from leaving?"

"Not one, Delsi. Not even one."

Chapter Twenty-nine

Delilah stared first at the pile of earth dug from the ground, and then at the deep, hollowed-out hole. Ronnie's bronze casket rested above it with two silk ropes draped underneath. Her mother stood on one side of her and Robert on the other. The only others at the gravesite were the funeral director and the minister from her church. He recited a number of prayers before opening his bible.

"I will read from Ecclesiastes:

"To everything there is a season, and a time to every purpose under the heaven:

a time to be born, and a time to die;

a time to plant, and a time to pluck up that which is planted;

a time to kill, and a time to heal: a time to break down, and a time to build up;

a time to weep, and a time to laugh; a time to mourn, and a time to dance;

a time to cast away stones, and a time to gather stones together;

a time to embrace, and a time to refrain from embracing;

a time to get, and a time to lose; a time to keep, and a time to cast away;

a time to rend, and a time to sew; a time to keep silence, and a time to speak;

a time to love, and a time to hate; a time to war, and a time of peace;"

"May the Lord take and keep Ronnie. May those left behind find peace and forgiveness. Delilah, only the Lord knows why this tender boy was called home. Mysterious is the Lord in his ways, and trust His wisdom, for it was the Lord who gave His only begotten Son to the world for our salvation. Find joy in your heart that Ronnie now sits beside our Lord and looks down upon us. Find joy that no pain consumes Ronnie's body, and his soul now lives in the spiritual realm. And find joy in the Lord's promise that you will one day join with Ronnie in Heaven and remain at his side for all of eternity. The minister then recited The Lord's Prayer. Afterwards he walked over to Delilah and took her hands. "May the Lord give you peace."

Delilah pulled her hands away and opened her purse. "I wrote somethin' for Ronnie."

The minister stepped back as Delilah unfolded the sheet of paper. She read it first to herself, and directed her look at her son's casket.

"My Ronnie, my boy
You runnin' free and fast now
I see you smile; it so wide

You my Ronnie, you my boy
I reach to touch you at nite
I go to the kitchen and make you food
I place it where you sit
Cause you still my Ronnie, you my boy
Been such a good boy to me
Such a good boy
You always be my Ronnie
You always be my boy."

One tear ran down Delilah's cheek. She wiped it away and slipped the paper back into her purse. No one said a word or moved from their place. Robert pulled out his handkerchief and wiped his eyes. A light rain began to fall. He opened the umbrella and held it over them, but Delilah did not feel the rain. Her eyes remained on Ronnie's casket until the dirt dug from the hollowed-out hole covered her boy.

CHAPTER THIRTY

The New York Times: *A breaking story from the Toronto Tribune claims that a meeting between the Canadian Prime Minister and former U.S. Senator Charlie Connolly took place earlier this week. According to reliable sources, the two discussed the possibility of American companies leaving the United States and relocating to Canada. Efforts to reach Senator Connolly have been unsuccessful.*

Charlie was in his office most of the night doing research. The information Michael Reny presented to him had raised more questions than answers. He researched every bill that Congress had presented to the president over the last four years. He detected a pattern where every House bill placed on the president's desk never received recognition or approval. These were bills written to help middle-class Americans. As Charlie thought back, he recalled that practically every speech the president had ever made was about helping the middle class.

At seven a.m. Charlie's cell phone began to ring and it did not stop. He knew the press was calling so he let the calls go to voice mail. One call showed Delsi's name on his cell phone. He answered it. "Guess you heard the news?"

"My phone's been ringing off the hook, too. They're asking where you are. Are you going to speak to the press?"

"Not yet. I plan to fly to Washington and meet with the president first."

"Are you going to tell him everything?"

"Exactly what Reny told us, and I have a few more questions for him myself."

"Should Robert and I go with you?"

"No. I need to be alone with the president when I ask these questions."

Delsi knew Charlie had something of vital importance to say to the president. If he wanted her to know, he would just tell her. "Okay, Charlie. Call if you need anything."

* * *

Charlie was stopped by the doorman when he entered his apartment building.

"I'm afraid someone's broken into your apartment, Mr. Connolly."

Charlie took the elevator to the sixth floor and hurried down the hallway. The door was covered with yellow police tape. He stepped through it to get inside. The living room was a mess. In his bedroom, his dresser drawers had been emptied, and suits and shirts were scattered all over the floor. He called Angela. "Are you all right?"

"I'm fine. What's going on?"

"I'm on my way over. I'll tell you everything when I get there."

"No, Charlie. I'm leaving for my parent's soon. Marcus is picking me up in a couple of minutes. We're stopping at Kaitlin's school to pick her up first."

"Angela, I need to see you."

"I need to be with my family right now. Marcus just arrived. Sorry, Charlie, I have to go."

The telephone went dead. As soon as the call ended and he hung up, the phone began to ring again. He recognized the number: The New York Times. He let the call go to voice mail.

* * *

Robert sped through the Holland Tunnel and crossed Manhattan to the Lower East Side. He took the Williamsburg Bridge to the Brooklyn-Queens Expressway and got off at Myrtle Avenue, where he weaved across Brooklyn and turned onto Lockhart Street. He parked in front of Delilah's place and locked the car. He knocked on her door and saw it open a crack. When Delilah saw Robert on her porch, she opened the door for him to enter. She motioned for him to sit down on the couch and she sat next to him.

"Why you here?"

"Well, I may be going away for a while, and I want to make sure you're all right." It was not easy to just walk away from Delilah after what they had been through together.

Delilah gave him a curious look. "Thanks for helping, but ya needn't worry 'bout mama and me."

Robert gave her an appeasing smile. His expression then turned serious. "A storm is coming, Delilah. I'm not sure how much danger it will bring, but it's going to leave a lot of people out of work."

"I got two jobs. The grocery and the cleanin' one. It gits me and mama through all right."

"Well, this storm I'm talking about is going to make groceries disappear off the shelves, and not all the people taking food will be paying customers. The grocery store people will let you go. So will the office people. Most companies in that building will stop paying rent, and some will close down altogether."

Delilah appeared confused. "How you know I won't have no job?"

"It's hard to explain, but a lot of jobs will disappear in this country. And with a food shortage I can't begin to imagine what will happen then." He reached over and took her hand. "Listen to me. If you and your mother stay in this neighborhood, you're going to witness violence."

Delilah's eyes widened. She got up and walked to the window. "It don't look like what you sayin' right now."

"Well, maybe not right this minute. But it's coming soon, Delilah."

She returned to the couch. "What should me and mama do?"

Robert hesitated before speaking. "I've made arrangements for you and your mother. Since you're an experienced cleaner, I found you a position on an estate in Westchester. You'll live in a small place there and report to the house manager. She'll teach you how to clean the main house." Delilah became uncomfortable, and then her eyes grew wide with fear. Robert had expected nothing less. He was telling her to leave her home and take a cleaning job at a place she had never seen before. "Don't be alarmed, Delilah. You and your mother will grow to like this place."

There was a t-shirt draped over the arm of the couch and Delilah picked it up and pressed it to her cheek. The shirt was Ronnie's and carried his scent. Her eyes looked at the ceiling and then around the room, as if she were waiting for something, anything, maybe a sign from him. "I can't leave my boy alone here."

Robert understood. Delilah felt close to him here. "Remember the prayer the minister gave at Ronnie's funeral?" Delilah looked at him with a sense of loss in her eyes. "It was a prayer from *Ecclesiastes* and there was one line in particular. *A time to get, and a time to lose; a time to keep, and a time to cast away.* The prayer doesn't mean to leave Ronnie behind. It wants you to find courage and to go on with life. Wherever you go Delilah, Ronnie will go, because you carry him in your heart."

Delilah dropped her head onto her lap and cried silently, but she could not hide her shoulders from heaving up and down. A long five minutes passed before she lifted her head. Robert saw a change in her. The expression on her face looked as though she had accepted leaving the only home Ronnie ever knew.

Then, Delilah became more frightened. "What if they don't like us, or I don't learn right, or break somethin'?"

Robert smiled. "They'll love you. It'll be just fine. And don't worry. Everyone breaks something at one time or another. The owners are wonderful people. The others who work on the estate already know you're coming. They can't wait for you to become part of their family."

CHAPTER THIRTY-ONE

The shuttle landed at Dulles International Airport. From there Charlie took a taxi to the White House. After walking through the metal detector, two security guards asked him to step to the side where they frisked him—a first for Charlie. He was escorted into the Oval Office where the president was sitting behind his desk signing papers.

The president looked up. "Charlie." He got up, walked around his desk and held out his hand. "Thanks for coming. You've been busy since leaving Washington. Care to tell me what you've been up to?"

"I'll get right to the point, Mr. President. The Fortune 500 are making plans to leave the United States. Their departure is imminent and I think you should know the reasons why they're leaving."

"Sounds like you've been more than briefed, Charlie. Didn't you negotiate the deal with Canada for them?"

"Yes, I did. In case there was the slightest chance of keeping them here, I wanted to uncover it. That's why I stayed involved."

"So then, how do we keep them here?"

"After listening to their reasons, I don't think anything can."

"Give me the bottom line on why they're leaving."

"They feel they're the sacrificial lambs and you're the butcher waiting for them in the slaughter house. Is that bottom line enough for you?"

"I get your point. We're running a deficit in this country of $1 trillion a year. Everyone has to pay their share. Do they expect the middle class to carry the load?"

"Their concern is that spending is much greater than the revenue this government takes in each year. Under your watch alone, Mr. President, the debt has risen over $6 trillion. The private sector doesn't see anyone trying to stop the bleeding. Their biggest concern is…" Charlie stopped himself.

"Go ahead. Say what's on your mind."

Charlie paused. "They don't believe a single dollar of their tax money will go toward paying down the national debt."

"Really? And where do they think the money will go?"

"Toward your vision for this country."

"Be more specific, Charlie."

"All right. Programs for the poor is one way to say it; redistributing wealth and turning this country into a social democracy would be more to the point."

"So we're back to conspiracy theories, are we? Every time I want to pull the poor out of poverty, I'm called a socialist. Well, if big business had it their way, everyone would receive minimum wage and no healthcare insurance."

"I'm not arguing with you, Mr. President, and I don't want to debate this, either. I'm here to tell you in person that these companies are leaving. You're the president and you need to figure out how to keep them here." Charlie watched the president's face for a sign, but he was difficult to read.

"What would you do if you were president?"

* * *

Delsi's cell phone vibrated and she saw Robert calling her. "Where have you been? I've tried calling you a dozen times."

"I'm afraid I've gotten myself into a pickle. Don't talk, just listen. The call is probably being monitored. I was pulled over coming back from my folks' place in Westchester."

"Where are you now?"

"I'm in Washington at FBI headquarters. After I was stopped, they drove me to Kennedy and flew me here. They've asked a lot of questions about Charlie and about you. They want to know if we're working with a foreign government. I told them everything they wanted to know. Anyway, they'll probably hold me another hour or so, and then let me go. I know you're waiting to call me an idiot for getting into this mess, so go right ahead."

"You're not an idiot, Robert. You're my best friend."

"Thanks for saying that. I...uh, Delsi, I need to hang up now. Someone's coming."

"Robert, don't hang up. Robert, are you there? Robert!" Delsi waited, but the line went dead."

* * *

"What would I do in your shoes, Mr. President? I'd call an emergency meeting with Congress. I'd tell them the United States is in imminent danger of imploding if these corporations leave. I'd assemble my cabinet to brainstorm as many ideas as possible to keep them from leaving. Then I'd get on the phone, contact the Fortune 500 directly, and invite them to Washington. I wouldn't let them leave until a deal was negotiated to keep them here."

The president sat behind his desk and thought it over. "Thank you, Charlie. I appreciate your advice. Now, if you will excuse me."

The president returned to his paperwork. Charlie waited a moment longer. "It's going just how you want, isn't it?"

The president looked up at him. He had a puzzled look on his face. "I'm not sure what you're talking about."

"You've confused everyone. Planned it perfectly. No one suspects a thing. Not even your staunchest opponents have called you out."

The president sat quietly and looked at Charlie. He stood up and motioned for Charlie to follow him out of the Oval Office and onto the White House lawn. "I'm still confused by what you mean."

Charlie was hit with the reality that he would need to share his deepest suspicions. "Let's just forget it, Mr. President. This is a bad idea."

"If it were anyone else, I'd say okay. But Charlie, we go way back, and you've piqued my interest."

Charlie walked a few feet away from the president and looked up at a window in the White House. The light was on and he could see a group of people inside talking and laughing. Charlie recognized one of the men. He did not recall his name but believed he was in the movie *Ocean's Eleven*. He turned toward the president. "I spent the night going over a great deal of information. Your inauguration speeches, State of the Union speeches, campaign speeches, and of course your campaign promises. The common theme was your support for the middle class. How big business hurts them. The devastation that Wall Street and the big banks have done to them. But every bill that's been presented to you that could've helped the middle class has been scuttled for one reason or another. Mr. President, your goal, as you tell us, is to preserve the middle class. Yet every day tens of thousands of them drop into the ranks of the poor. Since you've been in office, twenty-two million more Americans now need federal assistance.

"You talk about the job numbers you say your administration has created, something like five million, but filling the job of someone who's retired is not creating a new job. The truth is, Mr. President—and I'm pretty good at math—you haven't created one single job since coming into office. You give the appearance of helping, but when I look at your results, it's clear you haven't raised one finger to help the middle-class from sliding into poverty.

"I've asked myself how it was possible to get O'Boylecare passed, a bill few mortals could undertake without possessing incredible determination and resilience. But yet, you have not approved one other bill to help a suffering middle class."

"Now, Charlie, the health care bill got passed because our party controlled both the House and the Senate."

"Even so, there were many in your party that opposed the health care bill, but you dug in and went after them. You are, I might add, Mr. President, the most charismatic leader this country has ever elected into office. One by one, you convinced those on Capitol Hill to see your way of thinking. We all know your health care bill helps the poor, but my question is: Why haven't you used your incredible power of persuasion to get even one bill passed to help the middle class?"

"The opposition has blocked me at every turn. What can I do?"

"How is it that the best communicator to ever occupy the Oval Office has managed to become so hated by his opposition? And, those few times when a bill that could help the middle class was close to being passed, you managed to spoil its chances at the last minute."

The president did not answer. He stood and looked at Charlie.

"Here's what I think, Mr. President. The more people that slip out of the middle class and into the ranks of the poor, the more they become dependent on government. The more dependent they become, the more power you gain to levy taxes for the unfortunate middle class. You'll tell them it's corporate America's fault. They're the villain that has squeezed every drop of blood from the veins of Americans. Then you'll tell the middle class not to worry, though, because you're going to punish those evil corporations by taxing them more than anyone thought legally possible. You have exploited a downturn in our economy, Mr. President, and racked so much pain on the middle class that they don't see what's really happening. One morning, when it's too late, the people of this country will wake up to find the land they love has been transitioned into a social democracy."

"Charlie. No one could accomplish that even in a decade."

"When you're no longer president, Organizing for Action will take over and make you kingmaker for the next twenty-five years." The president's eyes widened for a split second. Charlie suspected he had touched a nerve. "It must give you some feeling of power to know fifty-five percent of the vote for the next election sits in your pocket. It doesn't get more powerful than that, does it?"

The president looked at his watch. "I hate to cut you short, Charlie, but the inauguration is tomorrow and I've got a house full of people to entertain, and lots to do."

"There's one thing more, Mr. President. Millions of middle-class people helped to elect you believing one day they'd have a better life. They believed in you, gave you their sacred vote. You took it and did nothing except watch them struggle to survive. Wages for middle-class workers have dropped six percent since you've been in office. Now, another sequester is brewing. How many of the middle class will lose jobs this time? A million, maybe two million? Every day seven thousand more people apply for federal aid. If this trend continues, by the end of your next four years in office, there'll be 70 million people on food stamps. I won't even begin to discuss the tens of millions that are applying for welfare. How do you sleep at night? Is this your vision of America?"

"You know very little about vision, Charlie. Unless you've carried one inside since childhood. Charlie, if the day ever comes that you get to live in this house, you'll learn a couple of important things. You'll want to do good, but those who despise you will rip you apart. When you extend your hand to find some middle ground between you and them, they slice it off at the wrist. Then, one morning you wake up and you realize there's only one thing that really matters: to win and to keep winning, and to do so at any cost. I know you had a dream as a little boy. Don't tell me differently, because we all do. And you also know it never fades from your memory, and you will do whatever it takes to keep your dream alive." The president took one step closer to Charlie. "What I do is for the people I love the most."

"Mr. President, what you've done is make a mockery of our Constitution. You've distorted the truth and lied to the American people about your intentions. Mr. President, I'm ashamed to say I know you." Charlie turned and left the White House grounds. On his way out he thought about what he had said, and it was appropriate to tell the president that he was ashamed of him. As for the president, it was clear by the look on his face that the accusations made against him were true. There would be no factual information to take before a Senate sub-committee, and malfeasance is always difficult to prove. All Charlie would be able to tell a sub-committee was that the president cared more deeply about one group of Americans over all other groups, and his lack of action on behalf of the middle class was his plan for turning the nation into a social democracy. Charlie would be laughed out of the Capitol if he ever spoke those words.

Charlie collected his cell phone and other property at the security desk. Once off White House grounds his phone began to vibrate. It was Delsi. She had left him a voice message. Rather than listen to it, he called her back.

"Delsi, what's up?"

"The FBI took Robert and he's being interrogated in Washington. They asked him about you and me and if we were working as agents for a foreign nation. I'm afraid they're going to hurt him."

"Okay, let me handle it. I'll get back to you." Charlie hung up and called the White House. "The president, please. Tell him it's Charlie Connolly." Five minutes passed while Charlie waited.

"Yes, Charlie."

"I'll be at Dulles to catch my shuttle to New York in one hour. I expect Robert to be waiting for me when I get there." Charlie hung up his phone and flagged a taxi. As he stepped into the back seat his phone rang again. "Hello?"

"Please hold for the Prime Minister."

Charlie waited impatiently until the Prime Minister of Canada came on the line.

"Hello, Charlie?"

"It's good to hear from you, Mr. Prime Minister."

"With all the press stateside, I thought it would be of importance to call as soon as possible and give you our decision. The Fortune 500 and all their people must be impatient at this point. So, without further ado, let me begin. We—the Parliament and I—have thought long and hard about selling off a portion of Canada. After much discussion, I'm sorry to say it would not be in our national interest to do so at this time. However, we have looked at the pros and cons of allowing the Fortune 500 to become Canadian companies.

It is something we welcome wholeheartedly. To induce them to seriously consider our offer, we are prepared to give them a ten percent corporate tax rate for the first five years, and then cap it at fifteen percent for the next twenty. Please let them know that Canada is prepared to welcome them with open arms under these conditions."

"Please hold just one moment, Mr. Prime Minister." Charlie reached into his coat pocket and took out the letter Michael Reny had given him.

Charlie, if you are opening this letter, it means the Canadian Prime Minister has reached out to you. We considered the likelihood that Canada would refuse to sell two of their provinces, as Parliament would find a contract such as this one difficult to sign. Only one option remains: their offer to allow the U.S. companies to become Canadian. If this is the case, corporate tax now becomes the negotiation point. If the Prime Minister agrees to reduce taxes to twelve percent for the first five years and cap it at fifteen percent for the next ten years, then you are authorized to accept those terms on behalf of the Fortune 500.

Charlie cleared his throat. "Mr. Prime Minister, are you still there?"

"Yes, Charlie, I'm here."

"On behalf of the Fortune 500, your offer is accepted."

"That's wonderful! I'll notify Parliament. There are plenty of details to work out…incorporating them as Canadian corporations, getting them listed on the Toronto Stock Exchange. I'm sorry, Charlie. I'm rambling."

"I don't mean to dampen your excitement, Mr. Prime Minister, but this is a dark moment for the American people. I want you to know that I stayed on this project for the sole purpose of stopping these corporations from leaving. Unfortunately, I failed to do so."

"Yes, well, under the circumstances, I can imagine your disappointment. I have another call coming in. We'll have to leave it there for now. So long, Charlie."

Charlie hung up as the taxi pulled into the airport. It stopped in front of the Delta terminal, where Charlie would catch the shuttle home. He noticed two black limousines stopped in the 'No Parking' zone. A quick look at the license plates told him they were government cars. Charlie walked over to one and knocked on the driver's side window. The driver opened the door and stepped out.

"I'm Charlie Connolly."

The man motioned to the other car and the back door opened. A large, burly man in a dark suit stepped out first. Then Robert emerged from the car.

"Charlie," he yelled. "What are you doing here?"

CHAPTER THIRTY-TWO

It was six a.m. when Charlie heard his phone ring. It was Delsi. She heard Charlie fumble the phone to his ear. She had just gotten off a call with Max Plummer.

"Charlie, are you there?"

"What time is it?"

"It's way too early to call anyone, but wake up. I have to tell you something."

"Hold on a minute." Charlie sat up and swung his feet onto the floor. "What's so important?"

"I just got off a call with Max Plummer. He tried reaching you all night, but you never answered."

"I needed to chill after the events of yesterday, so I turned my phone off."

"Well, Max reached me instead. He said that every border crossing into Canada is backed up twenty to thirty miles."

"How many border crossings are there?"

"A hundred and twenty."

"How could that have happened so quickly? I only spoke with the Prime Minister last night."

"It turns out Max has a good connection in Parliament. He knew early yesterday that the deal was going down, so they gave the Fortune 500 employees advance notice."

"How many are waiting to cross the border?

"Millions. But Max thinks it'll turn into a mass exodus."

Charlie was silent for a moment. "Okay. I'll be in the office soon. I'll see you there."

* * *

On her way to the office Delsi took a detour and stopped at the Tribeca Grand Hotel first. She walked into the lobby and approached the concierge. "Would you let Michael Reny know that Delsi is downstairs?"

The young man typed the name into his computer. "I'm sorry, Madam. He's checked out."

"Checked out?" Her mind raced. She started to leave, but turned back to the concierge. "Would it be possible for me to look in his room?"

"That shouldn't be a problem." He signaled the bellboy over. "Take this young woman to room 417."

Delsi entered the room and saw the bookcase was gone. The bed had been neatly made and the carpet vacuumed. When she walked into the bathroom she saw it was spotless. She had hoped to find a note, anything, but he had left nothing behind. On her way back down to the lobby, she recalled Michael's modus operandi of vanishing just before everything exploded. When working on the railroads in Brazil he had timed his disappearing act perfectly. And right before the miners revolted in the diamond mines of South Africa, he performed a Houdini act. Why should this adventure be any different for him?

Delsi was about to exit the hotel through the revolving doors when the concierge called out to her. "Excuse me? Did you say your name is Delsi?"

"Yes."

He reached behind the counter and pulled out a small package. "Mr. Reny left this for you."

Delsi ripped open the packaging and saw it was the first edition copy of *Steppenwolf*. It was the same one she had removed from Reny's bookcase the first day she went to his room. Inside the cover was a letter addressed to her.

Delsi:

I give you this precious and loving piece from my heart. I only wish it could equal who you are, and what meeting you has meant to me. You said I was lonely; you were right. You told me you have never felt love before. I, too, felt a wonderful sensation run through my body when we first touched. And, of course, the day you kissed me unashamedly I will remember always. You said you are capable of saying a word once and meaning it for all eternity. Well, I, too, could say that one word and make it last an eternity. Delsi, you have touched me more deeply than I can ever express in this brief letter. Please do not think my gift to you has any meaning as to my nature. It is quite the contrary. I am far away now, but had I stayed it would have been difficult for us. Charlie will need you more than ever now. And knowing your heart as you have allowed me to glimpse it, never would you desert him in this time when peril lay before all of you. And most of all, before a nation that needs the love and guidance only someone like Charlie can bring to this new beginning. As for us, who knows what the future may one day bring.

My Love,

Michael

CHAPTER THIRTY-THREE

Delsi arrived at the office early. She opened her computer and began to work on a new model. If Charlie was to make a run for president in the next election, she needed to calculate his chances. She already knew the numbers were less than great, but Charlie had to start somewhere.

As Delsi worked she began to wonder how it was possible for her beautiful country to have lost its way. How long would it take the people of this country to realize they had something truly remarkable here? How long till they are struck by the squander that led to her demise? Maybe one day, the people will join as one and work hard to rebuild her. Maybe then the people will no longer take freedom and liberty for granted. And no longer take whatever they can simply because she is a generous nation willing to give her all. So fragile was this beautiful lady known as our country, Delsi thought, and like so many other empires before, she disappeared in the blink of an eye just as Michael had predicted.

Robert walked into the conference room and tossed his coat on a chair before turning on his computer. Delsi and he exchanged glances briefly without saying a word, and they both began to work. Robert knew the amount of planning that lay ahead if Charlie expected to run for president. Robert would be tasked with keeping as many corporations as possible from leaving the country. He would also be the one to reach out to Congress and ask them to support Charlie—a daunting endeavor to say the least. Charlie would demand only the best from him.

Thirty minutes later Charlie arrived and went straight to his office. Delsi noticed the bounce in his step. When he looked her way briefly, he smiled. Delsi noticed his eyes were clear and energy radiated across his face. From inside his office Robert and Delsi heard Charlie whistle "America the Beautiful." They looked at each other and smiled.

"Would you two please come into my office?"

They walked in and stood in front of Charlie's desk.

"I was up most of the night thinking over everything that's happened this past week. I want to thank you both for your input. It's helped me to see both sides of what plagues this country, and I thank you for your passion." He laid a check down on his desk "Max stopped by earlier this morning and dropped this off. It's a check made out to me in the amount of $15 million. My first impulse was to refuse it. It's blood money, and I'd get sick spending even a dime of it. Then I came to my senses. The country will need every dollar it can get, so my share will be used to buy food, water, and for shelter. Tell me what to do with your share."

Delsi and Robert exchanged glances. "We don't want it either," Delsi said. "Put it with yours and spend it for a good cause."

"Done. I also made another decision last night. I'm going to run for president in four years."

"You could've blown me over with that announcement, Charlie." Robert said. He looked at Delsi and winked, and she smiled back at him.

"I thought it might come as a surprise. Delsi, I need you to prepare a model on the demographics. Tell me what my chances look like today and how we can stop the Backer O'Boyle machine from mowing us down."

"That's a great place to start, Charlie. I'll get right on it."

"And Robert, we need to reach out to every corporation that hasn't left the U.S. yet. Schedule as many meetings with them as possible. Then I want you to send an e-mail to every senator and representative in Congress. Tell them I'm holding a press conference at noon today to announce my candidacy for president."

"Backer O'Boyle's inauguration is today. A lot of senators and congressmen will be at his swearing-in ceremony."

"I'm aware of that. Now, I wrote a speech last night that I plan to give at my press conference today. I want your opinions on it."

Robert and Delsi walked around the desk and stood behind Charlie. They each placed a hand on his shoulders. They read to themselves as Charlie began to read aloud:

"Today, January 21, 2017 is a date which will live in infamy. Our country has suffered two tragic events: First, more than six hundred and eighty-six United States corporations suddenly and deliberately left our nation to find new residence in Canada..."

Delsi heard conviction in Charlie's voice. Finally, she thought, finally he was once again the Charlie of old. He finally shed what had been subduing him. She knew he would be stronger than ever.

"…Second, this nation is being stolen from its people. It is being torn apart and brought to its knees by divisive acts committed by those entrusted to protect our people and our Constitution. I ask Congress and every State Legislature to reenact the 22nd Amendment. Our Founding Fathers never intended for one man or one political party to control this nation. This is not what they had envisioned for future generations of Americans. I am now reaching out to the business community, the unions, the poor, the middle class, the wealthy, and the millions of young people who will inherit this land. As brothers and sisters we will gather around a large round table and reach an agreement on how to treat one another as we rebuild this nation. We must come to an agreement because we now face our greatest threat of all: the loss of our freedom and our liberty. It hangs in the balance and, once stripped from us, signifies these United States of America will no longer exist as our Founding Fathers had intended. Ralph Bunche once said: *With freedom comes responsibility.* We must live to this standard or our nation will perish. We will no longer be the light that shines like a beacon in the…"

Delsi drifted for a moment as Michael Reny entered her mind. He had told her Charlie would need her now, and he was right. Charlie had been given a choice: to lead the Fortune 500 into Canada or to do what he was doing this very moment. Michael knew all along what the outcome would be and it brought a smile to her face. He had also said she'd never desert Charlie in this time of peril. It came as no surprise that Michael knew her heart as well. As Charlie read his speech, a feeling of exhilaration rushed through Delsi's body and, for the first time in a long time she felt like an American again.

Richard Bognar's next novel *Catherine* will be released in November 2013. *Catherine* is a mystery/thriller about ruthless power, unmerciful greed, and the endurance of a love that transcends beyond the grave. *Catherine* takes place at a time in America when the supremacy of multi national drug companies is challenged by the emergence of an upstart biotech industry.

Catherine

Prologue

On December 16, 1999, three extraordinary events occurred that changed my life forever. The first took place while I was in the Brazilian Rainforest researching rare plants. Nothing I can recall has ever terrified me more than what occurred that afternoon. The second event—clearly the greatest tragedy to befall me—was the loss of my wife Catherine. As you will see, it began my search to find those responsible for the death of this most extraordinary woman. The third and final event of that ominous day is one that will take a great deal more courage to put on paper. But, I am compelled to tell you everything. My challenge will be to remember it all in the short time I have left. Let me begin.

CHAPTER ONE

It was six p.m. and, like clockwork, the jungle's darkness crept in, forcing daylight back. I had surprised myself, going almost the entire afternoon without thinking of Catherine, and not once recalling the promise she'd broken or that she was still in New York, thousands of miles away. What was she doing at this moment? Did I invade her mind as she invaded mine? Has she forgiven me for being selfish and for leaving? I had walked away from Memorial. What had stopped her from doing the same?

One bite more of mango and those thoughts faded. I lifted myself off a tree root, one of many that snaked along the black earth of the Amazon basin, and walked to where it tapered toward the river to drink. My shadow was cast onto the calm, dark water. For a moment I considered camping there. The place was peaceful, but I felt compelled to wring out every moment of daylight.

"Let's move out!"

Three Kayapo Indians rose from the jungle floor. I gripped my machete and began cutting a trail through the thick, green vegetation. We had a system: each man in turn at the lead, chopping until exhausted, when another then took his place. For a long twenty minutes I wielded my machete with as much force as the natives.

One of the Indians that spoke English yelled out, "Jack has *Loagi*."

A faint smile crossed the faces of the other Indians. I knew about *Loagi,* the god who enters the body of worthy warriors and gives them the courage to bravely fight their enemies.

"No," another Indian yelled, "no *Loagi*, much *Menpati*." All three Kayapo laughed at the thought of me drinking their favorite intoxicant, perhaps dancing through the night until collapsing from exhaustion.

A quiet breeze stirred patches of green-white orchids, and I avoided cutting those in my path. These elegant flowers reminded me of Catherine—a face oval and classic, with two hazel-flecked eyes peeking out at me, and, like Catherine's, flawed only by a wisp of bangs that eternally found their eyes, and beneath them, an intelligent gaze.

I was living my dream, having traveled to the deep jungle in search of a single plant that would heal just one disease. Impractical, yes, and my chance of discovering even a second-rate plant was remote, but I was living the dream, every researcher's dream. I pulled my shirt up to wipe sweat from my brow and a hand pressed against my back. It was Raoni, one of the Kayapo.

"Enough, Jack. Enough!"

Raoni was right. I was exhausted and stepped aside. Raoni took the lead and got to work, cutting our path through the plants with his swift, compact swing. He was my chief guide and friend, and we had learned to communicate with few spoken words. None of this surprised me. Raoni was brilliant, especially where plants were concerned. He was not formally educated in botany, but he understood the intrinsic nature of plants better than most trained experts. The jungle was his home, and like his father and grandfather before him, he found pleasure in the sanctity of this garden.

"Quiet!" Raoni lowered his machete and stood alert.

I stepped up beside him and we listened to the sound in the distance. His reddish-brown five-foot stature contrasted in every way to my larger frame and lighter skin color.

Raoni motioned for the men to sit. Then, in his sweet, high voice he said, "Chainsaws."

"Loggers? Out here?" People come to harvest trees, in particular, the valuable mahogany. Rapid changes were taking place in this part of the world, with the population exploding and new roads crisscrossing into the heart of the rainforest. What concerned me most was the rapid extinction of many of the rainforest's precious, indigenous plants.

"Why doesn't someone stop this? They're killing this world. Killing it!"

Raoni and the men stared at me with fear in their eyes. I shook my head and collected myself to focus on the impending danger. Harvesting mahogany trees was illegal, and some loggers had been known to dispose of a witness or two to avoid jail time.

We soon heard the sound of machetes cutting through the undergrowth. Raoni whispered something and the Kayapo men scrambled into the thickets. I scrambled as well. "Are they coming toward us?"

Raoni nodded.

I was about to give the order to retreat when the machetes went silent. Raoni motioned that the loggers and their Indian guides knew we were in the bushes.

"How could they?" I whispered.

He rubbed his finger across his chest and then under his nose. Somehow, from a distance of fifty yards or so, the Indians had picked up our scent.

Raoni stood up and yelled out in his language. I caught a few words about "jungle people," as he told them not to be afraid.

A voice yelled back, too quickly for me to understand. Raoni motioned to stay put while he spoke with the loggers. I tried to stop him, but he disappeared into the jungle. Then, for the first time, I removed a holster from my knapsack and buckled it on. It held a .38 Special. I ran after Raoni, but stopped when I saw him in a clearing some thirty yards ahead. "Get out of there!" My words were silenced by a gunshot and a piercing scream. Raoni clutched his stomach, spun around, and fell to the ground. Fear overwhelmed me. I knew that to run and aid him made me a target, as well.

A man stepped from the thickets and approached Raoni. He was Indian, and by the looks of his clothing, from one of the local towns. As he moved in Raoni's direction, I saw him remove his knife from its sheath. I pulled my .38 from the holster and took aim, uncertain if I would be able to squeeze the trigger. A doctor was committed to saving lives, not ending them. "Stop! Just leave him alone and go!"

We locked eyes. He studied me briefly and without a second thought continued toward Raoni. There was an explosion and both our bodies jolted. The echo of the blast beat through the forest. At first, the Indian stood motionless; then a look of surprise crept across his face. He stumbled to one knee and fell to the ground a short distance from Raoni. I lowered my weapon. My body began to shake. *This can't be real! Things like this don't happen.* Just as quickly, I regained my senses. There were more loggers in the forest and this was not the time to panic. I squatted under a rubber tree with leaves wide enough to hide me. *Catherine, thank God you're not here. Thank God you stayed home!*

The forest had turned silent. Was it possible one gunshot had frightened the loggers away? Were they content with the bloodletting that had just taken place? One of theirs for one of mine? Instinct took hold. *Just run and save yourself.* I looked to where Raoni lay face down in the clearing; he might still be alive. Twilight had now fallen and was the cloak I needed to pull him out. But once again, my instinct screamed, *flee*. After all, Raoni was probably dead. *Why risk my life to prove it?*

I crawled under a Jacaranda tree and waited, shivering, as dusk settled in. If Raoni was still alive, each moment counted. Finally, an adrenaline surge pushed me into the clearing where I took hold of Raoni and lifted him onto my shoulder. From the corner of my eye I glimpsed a mane of red hair. The man who owned it stood calmly with both hands on his hips. Two more men stepped into the clearing and flanked him. Their eyes were more intense, like predators waiting to pounce. I turned and hurried from the clearing.

The forest was dark and my thrashing had drowned out all other sounds, including that of loggers who might be chasing me. Raoni had begun to weigh me down and my legs were giving out. I stopped and listened for sounds of men in pursuit. Nothing. Had they abandoned the chase?

I laid Raoni on the ground and placed my ear to his chest. A faint heartbeat. *Thank God!* I opened my knapsack and pulled out a small pouch that held a scalpel and a pair of tweezers. Perhaps not the best tools, but better than nothing for extracting a bullet.

My objective was to locate where the bullet had lodged itself and then remove it without Raoni bleeding to death. In a hospital I'd grab a liter bag of intravenous solution and pump it into his stomach, wait a minute, then suck it out. If the solution had filled with blood, I'd know the bleeding was life threatening. There was no bag of solution or pump in my knapsack, so I had to rely on my instinct and guess right.

My next concern was infection; I knew the chance for it flourished in this place even though, when a bullet is fired, the friction of traveling through air sterilizes it. I gripped a penlight in my teeth and, shining it into the medical bag, I found the Alchonone, a greenish gunk. The sticky disinfectant would keep bugs from crawling into the wound. At least, that was my hope. I slipped on latex gloves and removed the scalpel from its casing.

"Raoni, can you hear me?" There was no response. *Good.* I made a four-inch vertical incision down his stomach. To hold the intestine in place, I pushed two sponges into the incision. I shone the penlight into the opening and probed. The bleeding was severe, and the jarring of his body while on my shoulder had not helped matters. I followed the source of blood to a ruptured artery, clamped it, and then searched until the light reflected off a dull metal object lodged in his stomach lining. I grabbed the tweezers and delicately dislodged the bullet.

I bit down on the penlight once more and threaded the suture. Minutes later the ruptured artery was stitched, as was the tear in his stomach lining. Even with perfect surgery Raoni's chance of recovery was slim at best. If the blood loss didn't kill him, an infection could, only more slowly and cruelly.

As I started to suture the incision, everything went dark. The penlight had died. "Damn it!" My hands probed Raoni's stomach until I found the outline of the incision. Stitch by stitch I began to close him up. There was a moan. *"Please, don't wake up now."*

Raoni's breathing became rhythmic again. I sutured the final stitches, bandaged the wound, and stabbed him in the thigh with a syringe of antibiotics. There was nothing more to do. I pulled a shirt from my knapsack and covered the wound. I leaned against a Caoba tree, still afraid the loggers might stumble upon us or that Raoni would awaken in the darkness to discover his belly had been ripped open.

The pounding in my chest was relentless and I took deep breaths to calm myself. Then, I closed my eyes. Catherine appeared, and with her vision came a twinge of pain. Her broken promise to come with me played throughout the night, until sunlight trickled through the braided Acacias. When the sound of tree animals began to scream morning into existence, I knew sleep was no longer possible. I removed the shirt from Raoni's wound and checked the sutures—not perfect, but they would hold. I rose to my feet, gently lifted Raoni and laid him over my shoulder.

The sun was due east. I followed it, knowing it would lead to the Kayapo village. Two hours later, Raoni lay in a hut with his family around him.

I returned to my bungalow where I found Brother Johanas from the mission waiting for me. He held a telegram in his outstretched hand.

"I took the liberty of reading it, Jack. Try to stay strong."

I looked at him, then grabbed the piece of paper.

Jack, sorry to tell you this by telegram. We failed to reach you by telephone at the mission. Return to New York immediately. There's been an accident. Catherine has been killed.

Colter Malone

ABOUT THE AUTHOR

Richard Bognar was born in Buffalo, N.Y. He attended Canisius College and received a Bachelor of Arts Degree in Philosophy. Richard and his wife Cynthia live on a small farm in Milton, Georgia.

You can e-mail the author at: rich@richardbognar.com

www.ingramcontent.com/pod-product-compliance
Lightning Source LLC
Chambersburg PA
CBHW021030130626
46552CB00005B/1771